So what happens now **Jennifer wanted to ask him.**

If it had just been about fulfilling an inappropriate youthful fantasy then she would be able to fully enjoy this moment and move on, but she could already feel a knot of anxiety beginning to form in the pit of her stomach. She wanted so much more than just a romp in the sack. But James was a man who moved on. It was his trademark.

So where, she wondered, did they go from here when they were positioned at opposite ends of the spectrum? Where exactly was the meeting point between a woman who wanted everything and a man whose relationships with women rarely lasted more than a handful of months?

Cathy Williams is originally from Trinidad, but has lived in England for a number of years. She currently has a house in Warwickshire, which she shares with her husband Richard, her three daughters, Charlotte, Olivia and Emma, and their pet cat, Salem. She adores writing romantic fiction, and would love one of her girls to become a writer—although at the moment she is happy enough if they do their homework and agree not to bicker with one another!

Recent titles by the same author:

THE TRUTH BEHIND HIS TOUCH
THE SECRET SINCLAIR
HER IMPOSSIBLE BOSS
IN WANT OF A WIFE?

Did you know these are also available as eBooks?
Visit www.millsandboon.co.uk

4

THE GIRL HE'D OVERLOOKED

BY
CATHY WILLIAMS

First published in Great Britain 2012
by Mills & Boon, an imprint of Harlequin (UK) Limited.
Harlequin (UK) Limited, Eton House, 18-24 Paradise Road,
Richmond, Surrey TW9 1SR

© Cathy Williams 2012

ISBN: 978 0 263 89099 0

Harlequin (UK) policy is to use papers that are natural, renewable
and recyclable products and made from wood grown in sustainable for-
ests. The logging and manufacturing process conform to the
legal environmental regulations of the country of origin.

Printed and bound in Spain
by Blackprint CPI, Barcelona

THE GIRL HE'D OVERLOOKED

PROLOGUE

JENNIFER looked at her reflection in the mirror. She had died and gone to heaven! Fantastic restaurant, fantastic food, even the ladies' room was fantastic. Beige marble everywhere and delicate little hand towels, a basket of them, to be picked, used and discarded. Could things get any better? Her cheeks were pink, her eyes were glowing.

She leaned forward and for the first time her physical shortcomings did not rush towards her in a wave of disappointment. She was no longer the too tall, too big-boned girl with the hair that was slightly too unruly and a mouth that was too wide. She was a sexy woman on the brink of the rest of her life and, best of all, James was out there, waiting for her. James, *her date*.

Jennifer Edwards had known James Rocchi all her life. From the small window of her bedroom in the cottage that she had shared with her father, she could daily look out to the distant splendour of his family home—The Big House, as she and her father had always called the Rocchi mansion, with its sweeping drive and imposing acres of stunning Victorian architecture.

As a kid, she had worshipped him and had trotted behind him and his friends as they had enjoyed themselves in the acres and acres of grounds surrounding the house. As a teenager, she had developed a healthy crush on him, blush-

ing and awkward whenever he returned from boarding
school, although, several years older than her, he couldn't
have been more oblivious. But she was no longer a teenager. She was now twenty-one years old, with a degree in
French firmly behind her and a secondment to the Parisian
office of the law firm in which she had spent every summer vacation working only days away.

She was a woman and life couldn't have felt any better
than it did right now, right here.

With a little sigh of pleasure, she applied a top up of her
lip gloss, patted her hair, which she had spent ages trying
to straighten and mostly succeeded, and headed back out
to the restaurant.

He was gazing out of the window and she took a few
seconds to drink him in.

James Rocchi was a stunning example of the sort of
aggressively good-looking alpha male that could turn
heads from streets away. Like his father, who had been
an Italian diplomat, James was black-haired and bronze-
skinned, only inheriting his English mother's navy-blue
eyes. Everything about him oozed lethal sex appeal, from
the arrogant tilt of his head to the muscled perfection of
his body. Jennifer had seen the way other women, usually
small blonde things he had brought back with him from
university, had followed him with their eyes as if they
couldn't get enough of him.

She was still finding it hard to believe that she was
actually here with him and she took a deep breath and
reminded herself that *he had asked her on a date*. It gave
her just the surge of confidence she needed to walk towards him and she blushed furiously as he turned to look
at her with a slow smile on his face.

'So…I've arranged a little surprise for you…'

Jennifer could barely contain her breathless excitement. 'You haven't! What is it?'

'You'll have to wait and see,' he told her with a grin. He leaned back, angling his body so that he could stretch his legs out. 'I still can't believe that you've finished university and are heading off to foreign shores...'

'I know, but the offer of a job in Paris was just too good to pass up. You know what it's like here.'

'I know,' he agreed, understanding what she meant without her having to explain. Wasn't this one of the great things about her? he thought. They had known each other for so long that there was hardly any need to explain references or, frankly, sometimes, to finish sentences. Of course, Paris for a year was going to be brilliant for her. Aside from her stint at university, which, in Canterbury, had hardly been a million miles away, he couldn't think of a time that she had ever left here and, however beautiful and peaceful this slice of Kent was, she should be champing at the bit to spread her wings and fly farther afield. But he didn't mind admitting to himself that he was going to miss her easy companionship.

Jennifer helped herself to another glass of wine and giggled. 'Three shops, a bank, two offices, a post office and no jobs! Well, I guess I could have thought about travelling into Canterbury...seeing what I could land there but...'

'But that would have been a waste of your French degree. I guess John will miss having you around.'

Jennifer wanted to ask if *he* would miss having her around. He worked in London, had taken over the running of his father's company when, in the wake of his father's death six years previously, the vultures had been circling, waiting to snap it up at a knock-down price. At the time he had barely been out of university but he had skipped the gap year he had planned and returned to take the reins of the company and haul it into the twenty-first century. London was his base but he travelled out to the country regularly. Would he miss having her around on those weekends? Bank holidays?

'I won't be gone for the rest of my life.' Jennifer smiled, thinking of her father. 'I think he'll manage. He has his little landscaping business and, of course, overseeing your grounds. I've been working to get him computer literate so that we can Skype each other.' She cupped her face in her hands and looked at him. He was only just twenty-seven but he looked older. Was that because he had been thrown into a life of responsibility at the highest possible level from a very young age? He had had little to do with his father's company before his father had died. Silvio Rocchi had barely had anything to do with it himself. While he had carried out his diplomatic duties, he had delegated the running of the company to his right-hand men which, as it turned out, had not been the best idea in the world. When he died, James had been the young up-start whose job it had been to sack the dead wood. Had that forged a vein of steel inside him that had turned the boy quickly into the man?

She could have spent a few minutes chewing over the conundrum but he was saying something, talking about her father.

'And it's just a thought but he might even enjoy having the place to himself, who knows?'

'Well, he'll get *used to it*.' But enjoy? No, she couldn't really see that happening. Her earliest memories were of her and her dad as a unit. They had weathered the storm of her mother's death together and had been everything to each other ever since.

'I think,' James murmured, glancing over her shoulder

and leaning towards her to cover her hand with his, 'your little surprise is on its way…'

Jennifer spun around to see two of the waiters walking towards her and felt a stab of sudden disappointment. They were holding a cake with a sparkler and huge bowl of ice cream liberally covered with chocolate sauce and coloured sweets. It was the sort of thing a child would have been thrilled by, not a grown woman. She glanced over her shoulder to James, and saw that he was lounging back, hands clasped behind his head, smiling with an expression of satisfaction so she smiled too and held the smile as she blew out the sparkler to an audience of clapping diners.

'Really, James, you shouldn't have.' She stared down at more dessert than anyone could hope to consume in a single sitting, even someone of her proportions. The awkward girl she had left behind threatened to return as she gazed down at his special gesture.

'You deserve it, Jen.' He rested his elbows on the table and carefully removed the sparkler from the cake. 'You did brilliantly at university and you've done brilliantly to accept the Paris job.'

'There's nothing *brilliant* about accepting a job.'

'But Paris…when my mother told me that you'd been offered it, I wasn't sure whether you had it in you to take it.'

'What do you mean?' It seemed rude to leave the melting ice cream and the slab of cake untouched, so she had a mouthful and looked away from him.

'You know what I mean. You haven't strayed far from the family home…university just around the corner so that you could pop in and check on John several times a week, even though you were living out…'

'Yes, well—'

'Not that that's a bad thing. It's not. The world would be a better place if there were more people like you in it. We certainly would be reading far fewer stories in the news-papers of care homes where ageing relatives get shoved and forgotten about.'

'You make me sound like a saint,' Jennifer said, stabbing some cake and dipping it into the bowl of ice cream.

'You always do that.'

'What?'

'Somehow manage to turn cake and ice cream into slush. And you always manage to do...*that*...'

'What?' She could feel her irritation levels rising.

'Get ice cream round your mouth.' He reached over to brush some ice cream off and the fleeting touch of his finger by her mouth almost made her gasp. He licked the ice cream from his finger and raised his eyebrows with appreciation.

'Very nice. Bring that bowl closer and let's share.'

Jennifer relaxed. This was more like it. Three glasses of wine had relaxed her but she hadn't been able to banish all her inhibitions. His treating her like a kid was probably going to bring them all back but clinking spoons as they dipped into the same bowl, exchanging mouthfuls of ice cream and laughing...

Once again she felt intoxicated with anticipation.

She made sure to lean forward so that he could see her cleavage, which was daringly on display. Normally, she wore much plainer clothes, big jumpers in winter and loose dresses in summer. But, for this date, she had splashed out on a calf-length skirt and although the silky top was still fairly baggy, its neckline was more risqué.

It was strange but, although she had no qualms about wearing tight jeans and tight tops at university, the standard uniform for students, the thought of wearing anything tight in front of James had always brought on a mild panic attack. The feel of those lazy blue eyes resting on her had always resulted in an acute bout of self-consciousness. His girlfriends were always so petite and so slim. In her head, she had always been able to hear his comparisons whenever he looked at her. Loose clothes had been one way of deflecting those comparisons.

'So,' he murmured, 'will you be leaving any broken hearts behind?'

It was the first time he had ever asked her such a directly personal question and she shivered pleasurably as she shook her head, not wanting, *under any circumstances*, to let him get the impression that she wasn't available.

'Absolutely no one.'

'You surprise me. What's wrong with those lads at university? They should have been forming a queue to ask you out.'

Jennifer blushed. 'I went on a couple of dates, but the boys all seemed so young, getting drunk at clubs and spending entire days in front of their computer games. None of them seemed to take life seriously.'

'At eighteen and nineteen, life is something not to be taken seriously.'

'*You* did when you were barely older than that.'

'As you may recall, I had no choice.' Jennifer was the only woman who could get away with bringing his private life into the conversation. She was, in actual fact, the only woman who knew anything at all about his private life and, even with her, there was still a great deal of which she was unaware.

'I know that and I know it must have been tough, but I honestly can't think of anyone who would have risen to the occasion the way you did. I mean, you had no real experience and yet you went in there and turned it all around.'

'I'll make sure that you're the first on the guest list when I get knighted.'

Jennifer laughed and pushed the plate of melting ice cream away from her, choosing instead to have a bit more wine and ignoring James's raised eyebrows.

'I'm being serious,' she insisted. 'I can't think of a single guy I knew at university who would have been capable of doing what you did.'

'You're young. Life shouldn't be about looking for a guy who can take the world on his shoulders. In fact, it should be about the guy who hasn't grown up yet. Believe me there's plenty of time to buckle down and realise that life's no picnic...'

'I'm not young!' Jennifer said lightly. 'I'm twenty-one. Not that much younger than you, in actual fact.'

James laughed and signalled to the waiter for the bill. 'You haven't done justice to those desserts.' He changed the topic when she would have had him pursue this tantalising personal conversation. 'I've always admired your sweet tooth. So refreshing after some of the girls I've dated in the past, who think that swallowing a mouthful of dessert constitutes an offence punishable by death.'

'That's why they're so skinny and I'm not,' she said, fishing hopefully for a compliment, but his attention was on the approaching waiter and on the bill being placed in front of him.

Now that the evening was drawing to a close, she could feel her nerves begin to get the better of her, although the copious amounts of wine had helped. When she stood up, she swayed ever so slightly and James reached for her with a concerned expression.

'Tell me you haven't had too much to drink,' he murmured. 'Hang onto me. I'll make sure you don't topple over.'

'Of course I'm not going to topple over! I'm a big girl. I need more than a few glasses of wine to topple over!' She loved the feel of his arm around her waist as they strolled out of the restaurant. It was August and still balmy outside. The fading light cast everything into shadow but the street lights had not yet come on and the atmosphere was wonderfully mellow and intimate. She surreptitiously nestled a little closer to him and tentatively put her arm around his waist. Her heart skipped a beat.

She was five ten and in heels, easily six foot, but at six foot three he still made her feel gloriously small and feminine.

She could have stayed like this in silence but he began asking her about Paris, quizzing her about the details of her job, asking her what her apartment would be like and reassuring her that, if it wasn't up to scratch, she was to remember that his company had several apartments in Paris and that he would be more than happy to arrange for her to stay in one of them.

Jennifer didn't want that. She didn't want him doing the big brother thing and imagining that she wanted him to take care of her from a distance so she skirted around his offer and reminded him that she wasn't in need of looking after.

'Where has this sudden streak of independence come from?' he asked teasingly, and his warm breath rustled her hair. He was smiling. She heard it in his voice.

They had reached his car, and she felt the loss of his arm around her as he held open the passenger door for her to step inside.

'I remember,' he said, still smiling and turning to look at her as he started the engine, 'when you were fifteen and you told me that you couldn't possibly get through your maths exam unless I sat and helped you.'

Never thinking that he had better things to do, just

pleased to be able to bask in his attention for a couple of hours as he had patiently helped her.

'I must have been a complete pain,' she said truthfully.

'Or a pleasant distraction.'

'What do you mean?'

'I was buried under work trying to fish my father's company out of its woeful state of affairs. Helping you and listening to all your school gossip often gave me a much-needed break from the headache of running a company.'

'But what about your girlfriends?'

'I know,' James said ruefully. 'You would have thought that they would have provided a distraction, but at that juncture in my life I didn't need their demands.'

'Well, that was such a long time ago. I can't even remember any of that school gossip.'

'And if I recall, you went on to get an A in your maths...'

Jennifer didn't say anything. The restaurant was only a matter of thirty minutes away from the house. In the blink of an eye, they would be back at the cottage and she would be able to show him that she really and truly was no longer the kid who had asked for help with her homework or filled him in on the silly happenings in her life whenever he happened to be down for the weekend. Maybe he wouldn't be entirely surprised...? After all, he *had* asked her out on a date!

She replayed that lovely feeling of having his arm around her and resisted the temptation to reach out and cover his hand with hers.

They drew up to the cottage in comfortable silence. Set in the grounds of the manor house, it was originally designed to house the head butler, but it had been annexed years before the Rocchis had moved in by a wily investor who had seen it as an efficient way of making some additional money. It was a happy coincidence that her father had bought the tiny two-bedroom place at around the same time as the Rocchis had moved into the manor house. Her own mother had died when she, Jennifer, had been just a toddler and Daisy Rocchi, unable to have any more children after James, had become a surrogate mother, bypassing all rules and conventions that predicated against two families of such differing incomes becoming close.

'Dad's not in.' Jennifer turned to look at James and cleared her throat. 'Why don't you…um…come in for something to drink? You barely had any of that wine tonight.'

'If I had thought ahead, I would have booked a taxi for us instead of driving myself.'

'Well, I know there's some wine in the fridge and I think dad's got a bottle of whisky in the cupboard. His once-a-month vice, he tells me.' She wasn't sure what she would do if he turned down her offer but he didn't and she breathed a sigh of relief as he said no to the alcohol but opted for a cup of coffee instead.

Inside the cottage, she switched on the lamp in the sitting room instead of the harsher overheard light and urged him in while she prepared them coffee with shaking hands. She was trying very hard to recapture the excitement and confidence she had felt earlier on in the restaurant as she had gazed at her reflection in the mirror and told herself that this *date* had arrived at just the perfect time, when she was still riding the crest of a wave, with her finals behind her and an exciting new job ahead of her.

She was so lost in her thoughts that she almost sent both mugs of coffee crashing to the ground as she turned to find James lounging in the doorway to the kitchen. Very carefully, she rested the mugs on the pine kitchen table and took two steps to close the distance between them.

Now or never, Jennifer thought with feverish determination. She had nurtured this crush for way too long. All through her time at university, she had tried to make herself like the boys who had asked her out, but her thoughts had always returned to James. His heart-stopping sex appeal and their shared history were a potent, heady combination and she had never quite managed to break free of its spell.

'I…I liked what you did earlier…' The palms of her hands were sweaty with nerves.

'You mean the cake and ice cream?' He laughed and looked down at her. 'Like I said, I know what a sucker you are for sweet things.'

'Actually I was talking about after that.'

'Sorry. I'm not following you.'

'When you put your arms around me on the way to the car. I liked that.' She slid her hand over his chest and nearly fainted at the hard body underneath her fingers. 'James…' She looked up at him and before she could chicken out she closed her eyes and tiptoed up to reach him. The first taste of his cool mouth sent a charge of adrenaline racing through her body and with a soft moan she kissed him harder, reached up to wind her arms around his neck as her body curved against his.

Her breasts were aching, her heart was beating like a drum. Every nerve in her body was alive with sensations she had never felt with anyone in her life before. Every kiss she had ever shared with other boys was drowned out by the scorching heat of this kiss. She felt his response as he kissed her back and that response was enough for her to take his hand and guide it underneath the loose shirt, up to the lacy bra that she had worn especially.

She was so lost in the moment that it was a few seconds before she realised that he was gently but firmly detaching himself from her and it was a few more seconds before it sank in that this was not a gesture preparatory to taking her upstairs. This much-longed-for evening was not going to end in her bedroom, making love while candles flickered in the background. She had agonised over her choice of linen, ditching her usual flowery bedcovers for something plain instead. He wasn't going to see any of it.

'Jennifer...'

Unable to bear the gentleness in his voice, she spun around with her arms tightly clasped around her body.

'I'm sorry. Please go.'

'We need to talk about what...what happened just then.'

'No. We don't.' She refused to look up as he circled round to face her. She kept her eyes pinned to his shoes while her body went hot and cold with mortification. She was no longer a sexy woman on a date with the guy for whom she had spent years nursing an inexhaustible infatuation. She bitterly wallowed in the reality that she was an awkward and not particularly attractive woman in a stupid, newly purchased outfit who had just made a complete fool of herself.

'Look at me, Jen. Please.'

'I got the wrong end of the stick, James, and I apologise. I thought...I don't know what I thought...'

'You're embarrassed and I understand that but—'

'Don't say any more!'

'I have to. We're friends. If we leave this to fester, things will never be the same between us again. I enjoy your company. I wouldn't want to lose what we have. For God's sake, Jennifer, at least *look at me*!'

She looked up at him and for the first time the sight of him didn't thrill her.

'Don't beat yourself up, Jen. I kissed you back and for that I apologise. I shouldn't have.'

But he had and she knew why. What man wouldn't suc-

*cumb to a woman who flung herself at him? It was telling
that he had come to his senses in a matter of seconds. Even
with everything on offer, she hadn't been able to tempt him.*

'You're young. You're about to embark on the biggest
adventure of your life—'

'Oh, spare me the pity talk,' Jennifer muttered.

'I'm not *pitying you*.' He stuck his hands in the pockets
of his trousers and shook his head in frustration.

'Yes, you are! I've been a complete idiot and I've put
us both in an awkward position and none of it is your
fault! Okay, so when you asked me out to dinner tonight, I
thought it was more than just two friends having a meal. I
fooled myself into believing that you might have begun to
see me as a woman instead of the girl next door! Instead
of the clumsy, ungainly, unappealing, borderline unat-
tractive girl next door.'

'Don't put yourself down. I don't like it.'

'I'm not putting myself down.' She managed to meet his
eyes without flinching although it cost her every ounce of
will power. 'I'm being honest. I've had a crush on you—'

'And there's nothing wrong with that…'

'You knew.'

'It was endearing.'

'Well, a pleasant distraction from when your pocket-
sized blonde bombshells were being too demanding, at
any rate.'

'You had a schoolgirl crush and there's nothing sinful
about that,' James told her with such sincerity that she
itched to slap him. 'But you're young. I know you said that
you're only a few years younger than me, but in terms of
experience we're light years apart. Trust me when I tell
you that in a year's time you'll have forgotten all about
this. You'll have met some nice lad…'

'Yes,' Jennifer parroted dutifully, wanting this entire

conversation to be over so that she could go upstairs and bury herself under the freshly laundered covers.

He sighed and shook his head. This was a Jennifer he didn't recognise. Gone was the smiling, malleable girl. Had he known that she had a crush on him? Yes, of course he had, although he had never openly addressed the issue. Now, for the first time, he could sense her locking him out. He understood but it was a strange sensation and he didn't like it.

'Your feelings for me are misplaced,' he told her roughly. 'I wasn't lying when I told you that you want to enjoy your youth with boys who are uncomplicated and fun-loving.'

'You make it sound as though I was looking for… looking for something more than just…'

'A romp in the sack?'

Mortified, Jennifer shrugged.

'You deserve a lot more than I could give you.'

By which, she thought, *you mean that there's nothing you're interested in giving me aside from a peck on the cheek every now and again and lots of good advice about how to live my life.*

He was being patronising and the worst of it was that he wasn't even aware of it.

'Don't worry about me, James,' she said with a forced smile, relieving him of the obligation to keep thinking about her feelings because he was a decent human being. 'I'll be fine. These things happen.' Two steps back, putting distance between them. 'I probably won't see you before I leave.'

'No.'

'Of course I'll keep in touch and I'm sure we'll bump into one another now and again.' One more step back.

'You'll be all right, will you?'

Jennifer chose to interpret this at face value and she looked at him with a polite, unfocused expression. 'Of course I will. As I told you, the job I'll be doing over there isn't going to be substantially different than what I've done over the summer vacations. Naturally, I'll be following through on a lot more and there'll be a great deal of translating but I'm sure I'll be able to handle it.'

'Right. Good.'

'So.'

James hesitated and raked his fingers through his hair.

'Thanks for dinner, James…and I'll see you…'

She remained frozen to the spot as he brushed past her, pausing fleetingly, as though hesitant to leave.

What did he think she was going to do? Jennifer wondered. Fling herself out of her bedroom window because he had rejected her? Was she so pathetic in his eyes that he doubted her ability to get over the slight?

The soft click of the front door closing signalled his departure and it was only once she was certain that he had left the cottage that Jennifer slumped.

She closed her eyes and thought of the excited girl who had bought a new outfit especially for her big date. She remembered her anticipation at having him all to herself over dinner. She had dreamt of seduction and of finally having this crazy crush of hers fulfilled. It suddenly felt like a million years ago and, although a year wasn't long, it was long enough to say goodbye to that person.

CHAPTER ONE

EXCEPT one year became two, which became three, which became four. And in all those four years, Jennifer had not once set eyes on James. Each Christmas, she had contrived to bring her father over to Paris for the holidays, which he had loved. What had begun as a one-year placement, during which she could consolidate her French, had seen her rise through the company, and as she had risen so too had her pay cheque. She found that she could afford to holiday with her father abroad, and on those occasions when she *had* returned to England she had been careful with her visits, always making sure that they were brief and that James was nowhere in the vicinity.

He had walked out of the cottage four years previously and she had fled to Paris, her wounds still raw. She couldn't imagine ever facing him again, and not facing him had developed into a habit. He had emailed her, and she had been happy enough to email back, but on the occasions when he had been in Paris she had excused herself from meeting him on grounds of being too busy, prior engagements, not well, *anything* because the memory of him gently letting her down remained, that open wound quietly hurting somewhere in the background of her shiny new life.

Except now…

She had nodded off on the train and woke with a start as it pulled into the station.

When she looked through the window it was to see that the flurries of snow that she had left behind in London were a steady fall here in Kent. The weather was always so much harsher out here. She had forgotten.

At six-thirty in the evening the train was packed with commuters and fetching her bags was chaotic, with people jostling her on all sides, but eventually she was out of the train and braving the freezing temperatures and snow on the platform.

She wasn't planning on staying long. Just long enough to sort out the problems in the cottage, problems she had learnt about via an email from James who had been checking his house in his mother's absence and had happened to walk down to the cottage to take a look only to find water seeping out from under the front door. Her father was away on his annual post-Christmas three-week holiday to visit his brother in Scotland. The email had read:

You can pass this on to your father, but I gather you're in the country so you might want to check it out yourself instead of ruining your father's fishing trip. This, of course, presupposes that you can interrupt your busy schedule.

The tone of the email was the final nail in the coffin of their enduring friendship. She had run away and, never looked back, and over time, the chasm between them had become so vast that it was now unbreachable terrain. His emails, which had been warm and concerned at the beginning of her stint in Paris, had gradually become cooler and more formal, in direct proportion to her avoidance tactics. It occurred to her that she actually hadn't heard from him at all for at least six months.

In Paris, she could tell herself that she didn't mind, that this was just the way things had turned out in the end, that their friendship had always been destined to run its course because it had been an unrealistic union of the inaccessible boy in the manor house and the childishly doting girl next door.

But now here, back in Kent, his email was a vaguely sexy reminder of how things used to be.

She wheeled her suitcase out to where a bank of taxis was only just managing to keep the snow on their cars from settling by virtue of having their engines running. Everywhere, the snow was forming a layer of white.

The water had been cleared, James had informed her, but there was a lot of collateral damage, which she would have to assess for the insurance company. He had managed to get the heating started. So at least when she arrived at the cottage, she wouldn't freeze to death. She hoped he might have left her some fresh provisions before he cleared off, on his way to Singapore for a series of meetings, he had politely informed her in his email, but she wasn't banking on it.

That was how far their friendship had devolved. When Jennifer thought about it for too long, she could feel a lump of sadness in her throat and she had to remind herself of that terrible night when she had made such a fool of herself. Someone better and stronger might have been able to survive that and laughingly put it behind them so that a friendship could be maintained, but she couldn't.

For her, it had been a devastating learning curve and she *had* learnt from it.

She gazed out of the window of the taxi but could barely see anything because of the snow. Deep in the heart of the Kent countryside, the trip, in conditions like this, would take over an hour. She settled in for the long haul and let her thoughts drift without restraint.

It had been a while since she had returned to the cottage for any length of time. She and her father had spent summer in Majorca, two weeks of sun and sea, and every six weeks she brought him over for a weekend. She loved the fact that she could afford to do that now. She knew that there was a part of her that was reluctant to return to the place that held so many memories of James, but that was fine because her father was more than happy to travel out to see her and she always, always made sure that she met Daisy, James's mother, for lunch in London when she was over on business. She had politely asked about James and given evasive non-answers whenever Daisy showed any curiosity as to why they no longer seemed to meet. Eventually his name had been quietly dropped from conversations.

To think of him moving around in the cottage made something in her shiver. Sometimes, a memory of the scent of him, clean and masculine and woody, would surface from nowhere, leaving her shaken. She hoped that scent wouldn't be lingering in the cottage when she got there. She was tired and it was too cold to run around opening windows to let out an elusive smell.

By the time they reached the cottage, driving was becoming impossible.

'And they predict at least a week of this,' the driver said bitterly. 'Business is bad enough as it is without Mother Nature getting involved.'

'Oh, this won't last,' Jennifer said airily. 'I've got to be back in London by day after tomorrow.'

'Lots of clothes for an overnight stay.' The driver struggled up to the door with the case, unable to wheel it in the snow.

'I'll be leaving one or two things behind. Clearing out old stuff.'

She paid him, thinking of the task that lay ahead. Aside from sorting out the cottage, she would be bagging up all those frumpy clothes that had once been the mainstay of her wardrobe. None of them would fit any more. In the space of four years, she had been seduced by Parisian chic. She had lost weight, or maybe, thanks to her daily run, the weight had just been reassigned. At any rate, the body she had once avoided looking at in the mirror now attracted wolf whistles and stares from strangers and she was not ashamed to wear clothes that accentuated it. Nothing revealing, that would never be her style, but fashionable and figure hugging. Her untamed hair had been tamed over the years, thanks to the expert scissors of her hairdresser. It was still long, longer even than it used to be, but it was cleverly layered so that the frizz had been replaced with curls.

The cottage was in complete darkness although the door was surprisingly unlocked. She lugged the suitcase through and slammed the door shut behind her, luxuriating for a few seconds in the blissful warmth, eyes closed, lights still off because she just wanted to enjoy the cottage before she could see all the damage that had been caused by the flood.

And then she opened her eyes and there he was. Lounging against the door that led into the kitchen.

The cottage hadn't been in complete darkness, as she had first thought. No, one of the kitchen lights had been switched on, but the kitchen was at the back of the house and the door leading to it had been shut when she had entered.

She literally froze on the spot.

God, he hadn't changed. He was still as beautiful as

he always had been, still the man who towered over other men. His hair was shorter than it had been four years ago and she could tell from the shadow on his jawline that he hadn't shaved. In the space of a few seconds, during which time Jennifer felt her breath catch in her throat, she took in everything. The lean, long body in a pair of jeans and an old striped rugby jumper, the sleeves of which were shoved up to the elbows, those amazing deep blue eyes, now focused on her in a way that made her head swim.

Disastrously, she felt herself catapulted back to the young, naive girl she had once been.

'James. What on earth are you doing here?' She knew that her hand was trembling when she hit the light switch. 'You told me that you would be leaving the country!'

'I should be in the air right now but the weather got in the way of those plans. It's been a long time, Jennifer…'

The silence stretched and stretched and stretched and she had to fight to maintain her self-control. Four years of independence, of cutting herself free from those infantile ties that had bound her to this man, and she could feel them melting and slipping away. She could have wept. Instead, she let the little ball of remembered bitterness and anger form into a knot inside her stomach and she began to get rid of her coat, which was heavy and damp from the snow.

'Yes. Yes, it has. How are you?' She forced a stiff smile but her heart was thumping like a sledgehammer.

'I thought I'd stay in the cottage until you got here, make sure you arrived safely. I wasn't sure whether you were going to drive or take the train.'

'I…I took the train.' Her car was parked outside her friend's house in London where she stayed every time she came back to the city. 'But there was no need for you to hang around here. You know I can take care of myself.'

'You've certainly been doing a very good job of that

while you've been in Paris. My mother frequently regales me with news of yet more promotions.'

She still hadn't taken a single step towards him because her feet appeared to be nailed to that one spot in the hallway.

He was the first to break the spell, turning away and heading into the kitchen, leaving her to follow him.

He hadn't said a word about how much she had changed. How could he have failed to notice? But then, why was it so surprising when he had never really noticed her? The ease she had once felt in his company was nowhere to be found and it was a struggle thinking of polite conversation to make.

'It's been a very successful posting for me,' Jennifer said politely. 'I never thought that I'd end up staying over there for four years but as I accepted more and more responsibility, the work became more and more challenging and I found myself accepting their offers to stay on.'

'You look like a visitor, standing there. Sit down. You might as well forget about getting anything done tonight. We can work on detailing what will need to be done to the cottage tomorrow.'

'*We?* Like I said, there's absolutely no need for you to help me with this. I plan on having it all finished by tomorrow afternoon and I'll be leaving first thing the following morning.' This was not how two old friends, meeting after years of separation, would act. Jennifer knew that. She could hear the sharp edge to her voice and, while she was dismayed by it, she was also keenly aware that it was necessary as a protective tool, because just looking at him rooting around in the fridge with his back to her threatened to take her down memory lane and that was a journey she wasn't willing to make.

'Good luck arguing with the weather on that score.'

'What are you doing in the fridge?'

'Cheese, eggs. There's some bread over there, bought yesterday. When the snow started, I realised I might find myself stuck here and if I was stuck here, then you would be as well, so I managed to make it down to the shops and got a few things together.'

'Well, that was very kind of you, James. Thank you.'

'Well, isn't this fun?' He fetched a bottle of wine from the fridge, something he had bought along with the food, she was sure, and poured them both a glass. 'Four years and we're struggling to pass the time of day. Tell me what you've been up to in France.'

'I thought I just had. My job is very invigorating. The apartment is wonderful.'

'So everything lived up to expectation.' He sat back in the kitchen chair and took a deep mouthful of wine, looking at her over the rim of the glass. God, she'd changed. Did she realise just how much? He couldn't believe that the last time he'd seen her had been four years ago, but then she had made sure to be unavailable whenever he'd happened to be in Paris, and somehow, whenever she'd happened to be in the UK, he'd happened to be out of it.

She had cut all ties with him and he knew that it had all happened on that one fateful night. Of course, he didn't regret the outcome of that evening. He had had no choice but to turn her down. She had been young and vulnerable and too sexy for her own good. She had come to him looking for something and he had known, instinctively, that whatever that something was he would have been incapable of providing it. She had been trusting and naive, not like the hard-edged beauties he was accustomed to who would have been happy to take whatever was on offer for limited duration.

But he had never suspected that she would have walked out of his life permanently.

And changed. And had not looked back.

'Yes.' Jennifer played with the stem of her wine glass but there was no way that she was going to drink any of it. 'Everything lived up to expectation and beyond. Life has never been so good or so rewarding. And what about you, James? What have you been up to? I've seen your mother over the years but I really haven't heard much about you.'

'Shrinking world but fortunately new markets in the Far East. If you like, I can go into the details but doubt you would find it that fascinating. Aside from the challenging job, what is Paris like for you? Completely different from this neck of the woods, I imagine.'

'Yes. Yes, it is.'

'Are you going to expand on that or shall we drink our respective glasses of wine in silence while we try and formulate new topics of conversation?'

'I'm sorry, James. It's been a long trip with the train and the taxi and I'm exhausted. I think it's probably best if you went up to your house and we can always play the catch-up game another time.'

'You haven't forgotten, have you?'

'Forgotten what?'

'Forgotten the last time we met.'

'I have no idea what you're talking about.'

'Yes. Yes, I think you do, Jen.'

'I don't think there's anything to be gained by dragging up the past, James.' She stood up abruptly and positioned herself by the kitchen door with her arms folded. Not only were they strangers, but now they were combatants, squaring up to each other in the boxing ring. Jennifer didn't dare allow regret to enter the equation because just looking at him like this was making her realise that on some deep, instinctive level she still responded to him. She didn't know whether that was the pull of familiarity or the pull of an attraction that refused to remain buried and she was not willing to find out.

'Why don't you go and change and I'll fix you something to eat, and if you tell me that you're too exhausted to eat, then I'm going to suspect that you're finding excuses to avoid my company. Which wouldn't be the case, would it, Jen?'

'Of course not.' But she could feel a delicate flush creep into her cheeks.

'Nothing fancy. You know my culinary talents are limited.'

The grin he delivered was an aching reminder of the good times they had shared and the companionable ease they had lost.

'And don't,' he continued, holding up one hand as though to halt an interruption, 'tell me that there's no need. I know there's no need. Like I said, I'm fully aware of how independent you've become over the past four years.'

Jennifer shrugged, but her thoughts were all over the place as she rummaged in the suitcase for a change of clothes. A hurried shower and she was back downstairs within half an hour, this time in a pair of loose grey yoga pants and a tight, long-sleeved grey top, her hair pulled back into a ponytail.

It had always been a standing joke that James never cooked. He would tease her father, who adored cooking, that the kitchen was a woman's domain, that cooking wasn't a man's job. He would then lay down the gauntlet—an arm-wrestling match to prove that cooking depleted a man of strength. Jennifer used to love these little interludes; she used to love the way he would wink at her, pulling her into his game.

However, he was just finishing a remarkably proficient omelette when she walked into the kitchen. A salad was in a bowl. Hot bread was on a wooden board.

'I guess I'm not the only one who's changed,' Jennifer said from the doorway, and he glanced across to her, his eyes lazily appraising.

'Would you believe me if I told you that I took a cookery course?'

Jennifer shrugged. 'Did you?' She sat at the table and looked around her. 'There's less damage than I thought there would be. I had a look around before I went to have a shower. Thankfully, upstairs is intact and I can just see that there are some water stains on the sofa in the sitting room and I guess the rugs will have to be replaced.'

'Have we finished playing our catch-up game already?' He handed her a plate, encouraged her to help herself to bread and salad, before taking up position opposite her at the kitchen table.

Jennifer thought that this was the reason she had avoided him for four years. There was just *too much* of him. He overwhelmed her and she was no longer on the market for being overwhelmed.

'There's nothing more to catch up on, James. I can't think of anything else I could tell you about my job in Paris. If you like I could give you a description of what my apartment looks like, but I shouldn't think you'd find that very interesting.'

'You've changed.'

'What is that supposed to mean?'

'I barely recognise you as the girl who left here four years ago. Somewhere in my memory banks, I have an image of someone who actually used to laugh and enjoy conversing with me.'

Jennifer felt the slow burn of anger because *he* hadn't

changed. He was still the same arrogantly self-assured James, supremely confident of their roles in life. She laughed and blushed and he basked in her open admiration.

'How can you expect me to laugh when you haven't said anything funny as yet, James?'

'That's *exactly* what I'm talking about!' He threw his hands up in a gesture of frustration and pushed himself back from the table. 'You've either had a personality change or else your job in Paris is so stressful that it's wiped out your sense of fun. Which is it, Jen? You can be honest with me. You've always been open and honest with me, so tell me: have you bitten off more than you can chew with that job?'

'I know that's what you'd like me to say, James. That I'm hopelessly lost and can't handle the work in Paris.'

'That's a ridiculous statement.'

'Is it? If I told you that I was having a hard time and just couldn't cope, then you could be the caring, concerned guy. You could put your arm round my shoulder and whip out a handkerchief for me to sob into! But my job is absolutely brilliant and if I wasn't any good at it, then I would never have been promoted. I would never have risen up the ranks.'

'Is that what you think? That I'm the sort of narrow-minded, mean-spirited guy who would be happy if you failed?'

Jennifer sighed and pushed her plate away.

'I know you're not mean-spirited, James, and I don't want to argue with you.' She stood up, began clearing the dishes, tried to think of something harmless to say that would defuse the high-voltage atmosphere that had sprung up.

'Leave those things!' James growled.

'I don't want to. Tomorrow's going to be a long day and

the less I have to do in the kitchen, tidying up stuff that could be done now, the better. And by the way, thank you very much for cooking for me. It was very nice.'

James muttered something under his breath but began helping her, drying dishes as she began washing. Jennifer felt his presence as acutely as a live charge. If she stepped too close, she would be electrocuted. Being in his presence had stripped her of her immunity to him and it frightened her, but she wasn't going to give in to that queasy feeling in the pit of her stomach. She launched into a neutral conversation about their parents. She told him how much her father enjoyed Paris.

'Because, as you know, he stopped going abroad after Mum died. He once told me that it had been their dream to travel the world and when she died, the dream died with her.'

'Yes, the last time I came here for the weekend, he was waiting for the taxi and reading a guide book on the Louvre. He said it was top on the agenda. He's been ticking off the sights.'

'Really?' Jennifer laughed and for an instant James went still. He realised that the memory of that laugh lingered at the back of his brain like the refrain from a song that never quite went away. Suddenly he wanted to know a lot more than just whether she enjoyed her job or what her apartment was like. She had always, he was ashamed to admit to himself, been a known quantity, but now he felt curiosity rip through him, leaving him bemused.

'You've opened up a door for John,' he drawled, drying the last dish and then leaning against the counter with the tea towel slung over his shoulder. 'I think he's realised what he's been missing all these years. He was in a rut and your moving to Paris forced him out of it. I have a feeling that he's going to get bored with weekends to Paris pretty soon.'

'We don't just stay in Paris,' Jennifer protested. 'We've been doing quite a bit of Europe.' But she was thrilled with what James had told her. It was a brief window during which, with her defences down, they were back to that place they had left behind, that place of easy familiarity, two people with years and years of shared history.

She glanced surreptitiously at him and edged away before that easy familiarity could get a little too easy, before her hard-won independence began draining away and she found herself back to the girl in the past who used to hang onto his every word.

'In fact, I've already planned the next couple of weekends. When the weather improves, we're going to go to Prague. It's a beautiful city. I think he'd love it.'

'You've been before, have you?'

'Once.'

'And this from the girl who grew up in one place and never went abroad, aside from that school trip when you were fifteen. Skiing, wasn't it?'

Yes, it certainly was. Jennifer remembered it distinctly. James's father had just died and he had been busy trying to grapple with the demands of the company he had inherited. He hadn't been around much and when, after the skiing trip, she had seen him for the first time after several weeks, she had regaled him with a thousand stories of all the little things the class had done. The cliques that had subdivided the groups. The quiet girl, usually in the background, who had come out of her shell because she was one of only a handful who had been any good at skiing.

'Yes, that's right.'

'And who did you go to Prague with?' James enquired casually. 'I've actually been twice. Romantic city.' He turned to fill the kettle and found that he was keenly awaiting her response.

Jennifer frowned. She was relieved that he had his back to her. Her first instinct was to tell him that her private life was none of his business. She quickly decided that it was one thing being scrupulously polite, but if she began to actively push him away he would start asking himself why and they would be back to the subject she was most desperate to avoid: her mistimed, unfortunate pass at him. He would really be in his element then, she concluded bitterly, holding her hand and trying to assure her that she shouldn't let the memory of it interfere with her life, that their friendship was so much more important than a silly non-escapade. She would be mortified.

'Yes. It's a very romantic city. I love everything about it. I love the architecture and that terrific feeling of a place almost suspended in time. Don't you agree?'

'So who did you go with? Or is it a deep, dark secret?' He chuckled and turned round to face her, moving to hand her a mug of coffee and then sitting down and pulling one of the chairs in front of him so that he could fully relax, using the spare chair as a footrest.

'Oh, just a guy I met over there.'

'A guy!'

'Patric. Patric Alexander. Just someone I met at a party a while back…'

'Well.' He didn't know why he was so shocked at this. She had always been sexy, although it was fair to say that she had never realised it. She was still sexy and the only difference was that Paris had made her realise just how much.

'French guy, is he?' James heard the inanity of his question and his lips thinned although he was still smiling.

'Half French. His mother's English.' She gulped down

her coffee and stood up with a brisk smile. 'Now, I really think it's time for you to head back to your house, James. I have unpacking to do and I want to be up fairly early to make a list of what needs doing. Hopefully not that much. I noticed that the rug in the sitting room's already been rolled. Thank you for that.'

'Thank God there's no carpet downstairs. The joys of flagstones when there's a flood! Why didn't this Patric guy come to help you?'

'Because he's in Paris.' She moved to the door and frowned when he remained comfortably seated at the table.

'The name doesn't ring a bell. I'm sure your father would have mentioned him to me in passing—'

'Why would he?' Jennifer snapped.

'Because I'm his friend…? How long have you been going out with this Patric guy?'

'I really don't want to be having this conversation with you.'

'Because you feel uncomfortable?'

'Because I'm tired and I want to go to sleep!'

'Fair enough.' James took his time getting to his feet. 'I wouldn't want to be accused of prying and I certainly wouldn't want to make you feel uncomfortable in any way…' He walked towards her and, the closer he got, the tenser she could feel herself becoming.

'I'm perfectly comfortable.'

'I just wonder,' he mused, pausing to invade her personal space by standing only inches in front of her, a towering six-feet-three inches of pure alpha male clearly hell-bent on satisfying his curiosity, 'whether you avoided me over the years because you were reluctant to let me meet this man of yours…'

'I was not *avoiding you* over the years,' Jennifer muttered uncomfortably. 'I thought we corresponded very frequently by email…'

'And yet every time I happened to be in Paris, you were otherwise occupied, and every time you happened to be in this country, I was out of it…'

'The timings were always wrong.' Jennifer shrugged, although she could feel hot colour rising to her face and she stared down at the ground with a little frown. 'Patric and I are no longer involved,' she finally admitted, when the silence became unbearable. 'We're still very good friends. In fact, I would say that he's my closest confidant…'

This time she did look at him and James knew instantly, from the genuine warmth of her smile, that she was being completely truthful.

The girl who had always turned to him, the girl who had matured into a woman he hadn't seen for nearly four years, now had someone else to turn to.

'And what about you?' she asked, because if he could ask intrusive questions then why shouldn't she? 'Is there anyone significant in your life at the moment, James?'

James was still trying to get over a weird feeling of disorientation. He tilted his head to one side, considering her question.

'No. No one at the moment. Until recently, I was involved with an actress…'

'Blonde?' Jennifer couldn't resist asking and he frowned at her and nodded.

'Petite? Fond of very high heels and very tight dresses?'

'Did my mother mention her to you? I got the impression she wasn't bowled over by Amy…'

'No, your mother didn't mention anyone to me. In fact,' she added with a hint of smugness, 'your mother and I haven't really discussed you at all. I'm just guessing because those are the sort of girls you've always been interested in. Blonde, big hair, small, very high heels and very tight dresses.' Jennifer couldn't help herself, even though dipping into this subject would be to open a door to all the insecurities she had felt as a young woman, pining for him and comparing herself incessantly to the girls he would occasionally bring back to the house. Amy clones. She took a deep breath and fought her way through that brief reminder of a time she would rather have forgotten.

James flushed darkly.

'Nothing changes,' she said scornfully.

'Really? I wouldn't say that's true at all.'

'You still go out with the blonde airheads. Daisy still despairs. You still only have relationships that last five seconds.'

'But you don't still have a crush on me...'

That softly spoken remark, a lazy, tantalising question wrapped up in a statement, was like a bucket of freezing water thrown over her and she stepped back as though she had been slapped.

What had she been thinking? Had she been so shocked to find him in the cottage that she had forgotten how efficiently he could get under her skin? She had managed to keep her distance so how was it that they had somehow drifted into a conversation that was so personal?

'That was all a long time ago, James, and, like I said, there's nothing to be gained from rehashing the past.'

'Well...' He finally began strolling to where his coat was hanging over the banister. She wondered how she had managed to miss that when she had walked in but, of course, she hadn't been expecting him. 'I'll be heading off but I'll be back tomorrow and please don't tell me that there's no need. I'll roll the other carpets. Get them into one of the outbuildings and keep them dry so that they can be assessed for damage when this snow decides to stop and someone from the insurance company can come out.'

'I'm sure that can wait,' Jennifer said helplessly. 'I won't be here long. I plan on leaving…well…if not tomorrow evening, then first thing the following morning…'

James didn't say anything. He took his time wrapping his scarf round his neck, then he pulled open the front door so that she was treated to the spectacular sight of snow swirling madly outside, so thick that she could barely make out the fields stretching away into the distance.

'Good luck with that.' He turned to her. 'I think you'll find that we might both end up being stuck here…'

With each other. Jennifer tried not to be completely overwhelmed at the prospect of that. He wasn't going to stay cooped up in his house when he thought that she needed help in the cottage. He would be *around* and she had no idea how long for. Certainly, the snow looked as though it was here for the long haul and the house and cottage were not positioned for easy access to handy, cleared roads. They were in the middle of nowhere and it would not be the first time that heavy snow would leave them stranded.

But maybe it was for the best. She couldn't hide away from him for ever. Sooner rather than later she would be returning to the UK to live. Her father wasn't getting any younger and she had enough on her CV to guarantee a job, or at least a good prospect of one. When that happened, she would be seeing him once again on weekends.

She decided that this was fate.

'You could be right,' she said with more bravado than she felt. 'In which case, thank heavens you're here! I mean, I adore Patric, but I have to be honest and tell you that an artist probably wouldn't be a huge amount of practical help at a time like this…'

CHAPTER TWO

AN ARTIST? Jennifer had gone out with *an artist*? James could scarcely credit it. She had never shown any particular interest in art, per se, so how was it that she had been enticed into an affair with an artist? And who else had there been on the scene? He was disconcerted to find that she had somehow managed to escape the box into which he had slotted her and yet why should he be? People changed.

Except, there had been something smug about her tone of voice when she had implied that *he* had changed very little over the years. Still going out with the same blonde bimbos.

He was up at the crack of dawn the following morning and one glance out of the window told him that neither of them would be going anywhere, any time soon. If anything, the snow appeared to be falling with even greater intensity. Drifts of it were already banking up against the sides of the outbuildings and his car was barely visible. It was so silent out here that if he opened a window he would have been able to hear the snow falling.

Fortunately, the electricity had not been brought down and the Internet was still working.

He caught up with outstanding emails, including informing his secretary that she would have to cancel all meetings for at least the next couple of days, then, on the spur of the moment, he looked up Patric Alexander on an Internet search engine, hardly expecting to find anything because artists were a dime a dozen and few of them would ever make it to the hall of fame.

But there he was. James carried his laptop into the sprawling kitchen, which was big enough to fit an eight-seater table at one end and was warmed by the constant burn of a four-door bottle-green Aga. Mug of coffee in one hand, he sipped and scrolled through pages of nauseating adulation of the new up-and-coming talent in the art world. Patric was already garnering a loyal following and a clientele base that ensured future success. The picture was small, but James zoomed into it and found a handsome, fair-haired man surrounded by a bevy of beautiful women, standing in front of a backdrop of one of his paintings.

He slammed shut the lid of the computer, drained his coffee and was in a foul mood when, minutes later, he stood in front of the cottage and banged on the knocker.

It was barely eight-thirty and so dark still that he had practically needed a torch to find his way over. Even with several layers of clothing, a waterproof and the wellies he had had since his late teens, he could feel the snow trying to prise its way to his bare skin. His mood had slipped a couple of notches lower by the time Jennifer eventually made it to the door and peered out at him.

'What are you doing here so early?'

'It's too cold for us to make conversation in a doorway. Open up and let me in.'

'When you said you were going to come over, you never told me that you would be arriving on my doorstep *with the larks*.'

'There's a lot to do. What's the point in sleeping in?' He looked at her as he removed his coat and scarf and gloves and sufficient layers to accommodate the warmth of the cottage. She was in a pair of faded jeans and, yes, she really *had* changed. Lost weight. She looked tall and athletic. She had pulled back her hair and it hung down her back in a centre braid. 'I hope I didn't wake you? I've been up since five-thirty.'

'Oh, bully for you, James.' The day suddenly had the potential to be unbearably long. He followed her to the kitchen, sat down and seemed pleasantly surprised when she began cracking eggs into a bowl. He hadn't had any breakfast. Great if she could make some for him as well. Did she need a hand?

'I thought you said that you had made sure to buy some food?'

'Oh, the fridge at home is stocked to capacity but I didn't think to make anything for myself.'

'Even though you were up *at five-thirty*? It never crossed your mind that you could pour yourself a bowl of cereal? Grab a slice of toast?'

'When I start working, nothing distracts me. And small point of interest…I don't eat cereal. Can't stand the stuff. Just bits of cardboard pretending to be edible and good for you.'

Jennifer had spent a restless night. This was the last thing she needed and she turned to him coolly.

'This isn't going to work, James.'

'What?'

'*This!* You strolling over here and making yourself at home!'

'It's impossible to stroll in this weather.'

'You *know* what I mean! If you think that you need to help, to get the rugs to the outbuildings, then that's fine, but you can't just waltz in here for the day. I have things to do!'

'What?'

'I have to clear some cupboards and I have lots of work to catch up on if it turns out that I can't leave tomorrow as planned!' She felt his eyes on her as she turned round to pour some eggs into a frying pan.

'It makes sense for us to share the same space, Jen. What's the point having the heating going full blast in my house when I'm the only person in it?'

'The point is *you won't be under my feet*!'

'I'm going to be doing some heavy lifting on your behalf today, Jennifer. It's hardly what I would call *being under your feet*.'

'I'm sorry,' she muttered with a mutinous set to her mouth. 'I'm very grateful for the practical help you intend to give me but—'

'Okay. You win, Jennifer. I don't know why you want to draw battle lines, but if that's what you're intent on doing, then I'll leave you to get on with it.'

He stood up and Jennifer spun round to look at him. Was this what she really wanted? To make an enemy out of the person who had always been her friend? Because she found it difficult being in the same room as him?

'I don't want to draw battle lines,' she said on a heavy sigh. 'I just don't want you to...to think that nothing's changed between us.' She flicked off the stove and moved to sit at the table. The past was still unfinished business. That clumsy pass had never been discussed and she had carried it with her for four years. The memory of it was still so bitter that it had shaped all her relationships over the past four years, not that there had been many. Two. The first, to a young French lawyer she had met through work, had barely survived three months and, although he had laboured to win her over, she had been hesitant and eventually incapable of giving him the commitment he had wanted.

Patric had been her soul mate from the start and they had had three years of being friends before they decided to take that step further. It was a relationship that should have worked and yet, try as they had, she had not been able to capture the sizzle, the breathless excitement, the aching anticipation she had felt for James.

She knew that all of that was just a figment of her imagination. She knew that she had to somehow find it in her to prise herself out of a time warp that had her trapped in her youth, but eventually she and Patric had admitted defeat and had returned, fortunately, to being the close friends they had once been.

He had laughingly told her that there was no such thing as a friend with benefits. She had told herself that she needed to find a way of blocking James out of her head. She wasn't an impressionable young girl any more.

James looked at her in silence.

'I know I…I made that awful pass at you all those years ago. We never talked about it…'

'How could we? You left the country and never looked back.'

'I left the country and then life just became so hectic…' Jennifer insisted. 'I suppose to start with,' she said, conceding an inch but determined to make sure that an inch was the limit of her concessions, 'I *did* think that it might be awkward if we met up. I *may* have avoided you at first but then, honestly, life just became so busy…I barely had time to think! I guess I could have come back to England more frequently than I did, but Dad's never travelled and it was fun being able to bring him over, take him places. It was the first time I've ever been able to actually afford to take him on holiday…' The egg she had been scrambling had gone cold. She relit the stove and busied herself resuscitating it, keeping her back to him so that she could guard her expression from those clever, perceptive deep blue eyes, which had always been able to delve into the depths of her. She couldn't avoid this conversation, she argued to herself, but she wasn't going to let him know how much he still affected her.

She was smilingly bland when she placed a plate of toast and eggs in front of him.

'I think what I'm trying to say, James, is that I've grown up. I'm not that innocent young girl who used to hang onto your every word.'

'And I'm not expecting you to be!' But that, he realised, was exactly what he had been expecting. After four years of absence, he had still imagined her to be the girl next door who listened with eagerness to everything he had to say. The smiling stranger he had been faced with had come as a shock, and even more surprising was the fact that his usual cool when dealing with any unexpected situation had apparently deserted him.

'Which brings me to this: I don't want for there to be any bad feeling between us, but I also don't want you thinking that because we happen to be temporarily stranded here, that you have a right to come and go as you please. You've seen to the little flooding problem in the cottage and I'm very grateful for that but it doesn't mean that you now have a passport to my home.'

'Point taken.'

'And now I expect you're angry with me.' She hadn't wanted to say that but it just slipped out and she could have kicked herself because, as the new woman she claimed to be, would she still care what he thought of her? Why couldn't she be indifferent? She hadn't seen him for *four years*! It seemed so unfair that after all this time her heart still skipped a beat when he was around and it was even more unfair that she inwardly quailed at the thought of antagonising him.

'I'm glad you said what was on your mind. Honesty being the best policy and all that.' He dug into his breakfast with relish. 'Did your father tell you that he's thinking of doing a cookery course? This, incidentally, is my way of trying to normalise the situation between us. Because you've changed doesn't mean that we've lost the ability to communicate.'

Jennifer hesitated, apprehensive of familiarity, but then decided that, whether she liked it or not, there were too many strands of their lives that were interwoven for her to pretend otherwise.

'He told me,' she said, relaxing, with a smile. 'In fact, the last time he came over, just before Christmas, he brought all his prospectuses so that I could give him some advice. Not that I would be any good at all when it comes to that sort of thing.'

'You mean being in Paris, surrounded by all that French cuisine, wasn't enough to stimulate an interest in cooking?'

'The opposite,' Jennifer admitted ruefully. 'When there's so much brilliant food everywhere you go, what's the point trying to compete at home?'

'You must have picked something up.' James saluted her with a mouthful of egg on his fork. 'This scrambled egg tastes pretty perfect.'

'That's the extent of it, I'm afraid. I can throw a few things together to make something passable for an evening meal but no one I've ever entertained has really expected me to produce anything cordon bleu. In fact, on a couple of occasions, friends in Paris actually showed up with some store-bought delicacies. They always said that they wanted to make life easier for me but, personally, I suspected that they weren't too sure what they might be getting.' She laughed and their eyes met for a few seconds before she hurriedly looked away.

There was no way that she was going to return to her comfort zone but this felt good, chatting to him, relaxing, dropping her guard for a while.

'And what about you?' she asked. 'Do you still avoid that whole domestic thing?'

'Define *avoid that whole domestic thing*.'

'You once told me that you always made sure that the women you dated never went near a kitchen just in case they started thinking that they could domesticate you.'

'I don't remember saying that.'

'You did. I was nineteen at the time.'

'Remind me never to have conversations of a personal nature with any woman who has perfect recall.' He had forgotten just how much he had told her over the years, superficial stuff and yet stuff he probably would never have told any other woman. 'Your father has been trying to lure me into cooking. Every time I've popped over, he's shown me one of his new recipe books. A few months ago I came for a few days to oversee some work my mother was having done in the house, and your father asked us both to dinner here. We were treated to an array of exotic meals and I was personally given a lecture on the importance of a man having interests outside work. Have you any idea how difficult it is for a man to defend himself from a dual-pronged attack? Your father preached to me about learning to enjoy my leisure time and my mother made significant noises about the correlation between hard work and high blood pressure.'

Jennifer laughed again, that rich, full-bodied laugh that reminded James of how much he had missed her uncomplicated company over the years. Except now...nothing was as uncomplicated as it once was. They could skim the surface with small talk and reach a place in which they both felt comfortable, but he realised that he wanted to dig deeper. He didn't want to just harp back to the good old days. He didn't want to just keep it light.

'I thought I'd see if that Patric guy of yours had a presence on the Internet.' He changed the subject, standing up and waving her to sit back down when she would have helped him clear the table.

Jennifer went still. Why, she wanted to ask, would he do that?

'Oh?'

'He's well reviewed.'

'Why would you want to check up on him?' she asked abruptly. 'Did you think that I was lying? Made him up?'

'Of course I didn't!' He shook his head in frustration as they teetered back to square one after their fragile truce.

'Then what? Why the curiosity?'

He looked at her closed, uninviting expression and scowled. She might have loosened up for a few minutes, but the bottom line was she wanted their relationship to remain on the safe, one-dimensional plane it had always occupied.

He thought back to that crossroads moment, when, four years ago, she had offered herself to him. Hell, he could still taste her mouth on his before he had gently pushed her away. In fact, thinking about it, he wondered whether he had ever really put it behind him.

'Call it human nature,' he gritted. 'Is it a taboo subject? Am I getting too close to showing a perfectly normal interest in the person you are *now*?'

Jennifer couldn't argue with that. *She* was the one at fault. It was only natural that he would want to exchange more than just polite pleasantries about their past or idle chit-chat about their parents. It wasn't his fault that she felt threatened whenever she thought about him getting too close and the reason she felt threatened was because she still had feelings for him. She didn't know what exactly those feelings were, but they were defining the way she responded. It was crazy.

It was going to be very tiring if they continually veered between harmless small talk and bitter arguments. Worse, he would wonder why.

'Patric isn't a taboo subject. I just think that I already told you everything there is to know about him, and what I didn't you probably gleaned from the Internet. He's a big name in Europe. Or at least, he soon will be. His last exhibition was a huge success. Everything sold and he has a number of galleries vying to show his work.'

James had read all of that in the glowing article on the computer. They had not stinted in their praise.

'You were never into art.'

'I...I...never really thought that it would be something practical to do so I dropped it at school and really, around here...well, museums and art galleries aren't a dime a dozen. I think I started realising how much I loved art when I went to university...so it was easy to fall in love with it in Paris where it's all around you...'

'And the French guy was all part and parcel of the falling-in-love process?'

Jennifer shrugged. 'We were close friends first. Maybe I got caught up in his passion and enthusiasm over the years. I don't know.'

'And it didn't work out in the end.'

'No. It didn't. Now, why don't you start getting the rugs together and I'll give you a hand? There's a great wad of tarpaulin in the coal shed at the back of the cottage. If I get that, then we can cover the rugs and hopefully they won't get too wet when we lug them over.'

What little personal conversation she had submitted to was over. James was receiving that message loud and clear. He had never been one to encourage touching confidences from women. Events in his past had conspired to put a cynical spin on every relationship he had, although that was something he kept to himself. It was weird that he was now increasingly curious to find out more about Jennifer. It was almost as though he had suddenly discovered that his faithful pet could spout poetry and speak four languages.

He wondered whether his sudden interest was a result of being marooned with her by the snow, compounded by the fact that he hadn't seen her in years. Had he met her at his mother's house, would they have skirted over the same ground, played their usual roles and then parted company to meet again in three weeks' time and repeat the process?

Hauling rugs into an outbuilding seemed an inadequate substitute to having his curiosity sated, but he dropped the subject and, for the next couple of hours, they worked alongside each other in amicable companionship, exchanging opinions on what would and wouldn't need to be done to the cottage. It was an old place and prone to all the symptoms of old age. Things needed replacing on a frequent basis and an updating process was long overdue.

'Right,' Jennifer said, once they were back in the cottage. 'You're going to have to go now, James.'

The past couple of hours were a warning to her that she had to be careful around him. She had always found his charm, his wit, his intelligence, irresistible and time, it appeared, had not diminished his appeal in that area. He could still make her laugh, and wading through the fast-falling snow was a great deal safer than sitting in a cosy kitchen where they had eye-to-eye contact.

What alarmed her were those casual touches, the brush of his gloved fingers against her arm, the feel of his thigh next to hers as they had manoeuvred the rug into the out-building, laughing and looking at the collection of junk they had had to shift to make room.

Her body had felt alive; her skin had tingled. She had been that twenty-one-year-old girl again, yearning to be touched. At least, it had felt like that. What if this whole unforeseen situation, trapped in the snow, made her do something regrettable? It was barely a thought that she allowed to cross her mind, but she knew that it was there, like an ugly monster shifting lazily underneath the de-fences she had laboured to pile on top of it. What if, on the spur of the moment, she let her hand linger just a little bit too long on his arm? What if she held his look for too long?

He was no longer the cardboard cut-out hero of her youth. She had moved on from blind infatuation and now, here, she was beginning to see the complex man who told her how tough it was moving from being a carefree stu-dent to a man who needed to run a company. He shared thoughts about his mother, getting older and living in a house that was too big for her, and she could see the worry etched on his face.

She didn't like it or perhaps, scarily, she liked it too much. He was easy and relaxed with her because he still considered her a friend. She was wary with him and she had to be because, beyond any friendship, there were still feelings buried there and they frightened her.

So spending the afternoon in the cottage together, be-cause *it made sense*, just wasn't going to do.

'I have some clothes I need to box up and also some work to do because, you're right, it doesn't look likely that

I'm going to make it back to London tomorrow. In fact, I'll be lucky if I get out of here by the weekend. So…'

Neither of them had had a chance to change and her hair was damp from the falling snow. Dark tendrils curled around her face. Her cheeks were pink from the cold and the woollen hat she had put on was pulled down low, almost down to her eyes, huge and brown and staring purposefully at him. Unlike the babes he dated, she had a dramatic, intelligent face, a face he found he liked looking at.

'I can't think of the last time I was chucked out of a woman's house,' he said, raising his eyebrows. 'Come to think of it, I can't think of the last time I did anything manual with a woman.'

'I doubt any of your girlfriends would be any good in conditions like these. Deep snow and kitten heels don't go well together. And I'm not a woman, I'm a friend.'

'Thanks for reminding me,' James murmured. 'I was in danger of forgetting…'

Jennifer drew in a shaky breath. What did that mean? No. She refused to waste time speculating on the things he said and reading meanings into throwaway remarks. She knew from experience that that was a road that led nowhere and, anyway, she *didn't care about him*. She had spent *four years* putting him behind her!

'Perhaps later this evening we can share a quick meal. Or I could come up to the house. It *does* seem silly for us to eat on our own when we could join rations.'

'And I could cook for you.' His voice was warm and amused. 'Adding yet something else to the steadily growing list of things I don't do with women but I do for you.'

Was he flirting with her? 'You can if you want to,' she countered sharply, 'but if not you're more than welcome to come here and have something with me or we could just reconvene in the morning and take it from there. You have my mobile number, don't you?'

'I think it's one of the things you omitted to give me when you left…' Once upon a time his charm would have swept her off her feet. Now, it slid off her, leaving her unaffected. In fact, leaving her irritated.

'Then let's exchange mobile numbers now just in case there's a change of plan. If I find that I'm behind with all the stuff I want to do, then I'll contact you.'

'And are you going to get in touch with John and let him know what's happened?'

'No.' Tell her father? That she was holed up in the cottage in the middle of a snowstorm with James? His imagination would be on overdrive if she did that! He had been all too aware of her childish crush! She had been so young and disingenuous…incapable of hiding her emotions, wearing her heart on her sleeve like any impressionable teenager. He had never known about that disastrous final dinner she had had with James. At least, he had never known the details but he was as sharp as a tack. He had known that it hadn't lived up to expectations because the following day she had been quiet, avoiding his questions. And then she had left for Paris and never seen James again. 'No. You were right to get in touch with me and leave Dad out of this. He doesn't get to see Anthony often and he looks forward to his three-week holiday up there. Anyway, the transport links are terrible at the moment. He would have a hard time returning and there's nothing he can do here that I can't manage.'

'How does it feel?' James asked softly and she stared at him with a perplexed frown.

'What are you talking about?'

'To be in charge.'

'I'm not in charge of anything,' Jennifer mumbled,

dipping her head. She wondered whether it was a compliment to be seen as a woman *in charge*. Maybe from someone else it would have been, but from James…? 'Well, maybe I *am* in charge,' she amended, refusing to be drawn into thinking that there was something wrong with not being a helpless feeble woman incapable of doing anything useful in case a nail got chipped. 'Dad's not getting any younger. He's going to be sixty-eight on his next birthday and he's been complaining about tiring more easily. He jokes about it, but I can tell from when we've been walking around Paris that he's not as spritely as he used to be.'

'And where does that leave you, I wonder?'

'I'm not saying that Dad has suddenly become old and feeble!'

'I'm curious as to how long you intend to work in Paris…'

'That's a big subject for us to suddenly start discussing,' Jennifer said, fighting the irresistible temptation to confide. Patric might be a wonderful friend and a sympathetic confidant, but he wasn't James. James who had known her for most of her life and who knew her father better than anyone else.

'Is it?' He shrugged and shot her a crooked smile. 'Am I stepping too close to something personal?'

'Of course not,' Jennifer said uncomfortably, hating the way he found it so easy to return to their familiarity while she continued to fight against it tooth and nail because in her head it represented a retrograde step. 'I…yes, I've been thinking about that, wondering whether it might not be time to return to England…'

'But you're worried that you've settled into a lifestyle that agrees with you and you might just get back here and have difficulty slotting back in. This isn't Paris.'

'I've made a lot of friends,' Jennifer said defensively.

'I know the work and I'm very well paid… I don't even know whether I'd be able to find a similar job over here! I keep abreast of the news. There are no jobs!'

'Plus you hate change and the biggest thing you've ever done is go to Paris and reinvent yourself…'

'Stop trying to shove me back in time. I'm not that person any more.' But yes, she had never liked change even though she had never had a problem adapting to different circumstances. Secondary school had been a challenge, but she had done it and it had been fine. University, likewise. However, she had had no choice in either of those. Paris, as he had said, had been her big step. Returning to England would be another.

'No, you're not,' James said quietly, while she continued to glare at him. 'I would have no problem giving you a job, Jennifer. There are a lot of opportunities in my company for someone fluent in French with the level of experience you've had. In fact, I have access to a number of company apartments. It would be an easy matter for me to sort one of them out for you…'

'No, thank you!' Jennifer could think of nothing worse than breaking out of her comfort zone only to be reduced to handouts from James Rocchi. In Paris, she had been her own person. She shuddered to think how it would be if she were to be working in his company and renting one of his apartments. Would he be dropping in every two minutes with one of his blonde Barbies on his arm to check up on her and make sure that she was okay? Nosing into her private life and expressing surprise if she happened to be dating someone? Maybe looking up this, as yet, fictitious someone on the Internet so that he could check for himself that she wasn't dating someone unsuitable? Or maybe just checking out of curiosity, the way he had with Patric?

'I mean,' she amended hurriedly, 'that's a generous

offer but I haven't made any decisions as to whether or not I'll be returning just yet, anyway. And when I *do* decide to return...well, I would want to find my own way. I'm sure my boss in Paris will supply me with excellent references...'

James tried not to scowl as she smiled brightly at him, a big, glassy smile that set his teeth on edge. He was so used to her malleability! Now, in receipt of this polite dismissal, he felt strangely impotent and piqued.

'I'm sure he would.'

'And I've managed to save quite a bit while I've been over there. I stayed in a company flat and they kindly let me carry on there at a very subsidised rate after my one-year secondment was at an end. In fact, I would probably be able to put down a deposit on a small place of my own after a while. Not in London, of course. I would have to travel in. But definitely in Kent somewhere. I could work in London, because that's where the jobs are, and commute like most people have to do. So...thanks for the offer of one of your company flats, but there's no need to feel duty-bound to be charitable.'

'And on that note, I think I'll leave.'

She let him. She saw him to the door, where they made polite noises about the continuing bad weather. He suggested that he come over to the cottage to eat because it would be easier for him to tackle the short distance in blizzard conditions; he was sure he had a pair of skis lurking in a cupboard somewhere from his heady teenage years. She smiled blandly.

Inside it felt so wrong to be closing the door on him with this undercurrent of ill feeling between them.

Her head was telling her to let go of the past and find new ground with him, as he obviously wanted to do with her. New, inoffensive ground. Her heart, however, was beating to a different tune.

She spent the remainder of the day clearing out cupboards and bagging old clothes. She couldn't believe the rubbish she pulled out of her wardrobe. The cottage was small and yet the cupboard in her bedroom was like the wardrobe in Narnia—never ending. She had binned the outfit she had worn all those years ago on their disastrous dinner date in a fit of humiliation and hurt, but the shoes were still there, stuffed at the back, and she pulled them out and relived that night all over again.

Then she worked on her computer. She didn't know how long the connection would last. Paris seemed like a million light years away and when she managed to talk to Patric, she found it hard to imagine that she had once thought that he might be the one for her.

She tried not to look at the clock and told herself that she honestly didn't care whether James came over to the cottage for dinner or not. Yes, sure, some adult company would be nice. Eating pasta for one while the snow bucketed down outside was a pretty lonely prospect. She told herself that she likewise didn't care if he had taken offence at her rejection of his offer of a job and a place to rent. She could have handled it differently, but the message would have amounted to the same thing whatever. On both counts, she knew that she was kidding herself. She was keyed up to see him later. Like an addict drawn to the source of her addiction, she craved the way he made her feel.

By six, she was glancing at the clock on the mantelpiece, and when her mobile vibrated next to her on the sofa, she had to fight back the disappointment at the thought that he would be at the other end of the line informing her that he had decided to give their arrangement a miss.

CHAPTER THREE

'IF YOU'RE calling to tell me that you won't be coming over tonight for dinner, then don't worry about it. Not a problem. I still have so much work to do, anyway! You wouldn't believe it! Plus I'm going to take the opportunity to catch up with some of my frie...'

'Jennifer, shut up.'

'How dare you?'

'You need to do exactly what I say. Get dressed in some warm clothes, come out of your cottage and head for the copse behind it. You know the one I mean.'

'James, what's going on? You're scaring me.'

'I've had a bit of an accident.'

'You...*what*?' Jennifer stood up, felt giddy and immediately sat back down. Every nerve in her body had gone into sudden, panicked overdrive. 'What do you mean?'

'There were some high winds here a couple of days ago. Just before you came. Some fallen branches in the copse behind the cottage and a tree that's about to go and is dangerously close to one of the overhead cables.'

'You tripped over a branch on your way here?'

'Don't be ridiculous! How feeble do you think I am? After I left you earlier, I got back to the house, did some work and then thought that I might as well see if I could bring the tree down, get it clear of the overhead power lines.'

In a flashback springing from nowhere, she had a vivid memory of him as a young boy not yet sixteen, strapped halfway up one of the towering trees that bordered the house, chainsaw in one hand, reaching for a branch that had broken, while underneath his parents yelled for him to get down *immediately*. He had grown up in sprawling acres of deepest countryside and had always loved getting involved in the hard work of running the estate. He had had a reckless disregard for personal safety, had loved challenging himself. She had adored that about him.

'I can't believe you could have been so stupid!' she yelled down the phone. 'You're not sixteen any more, James! Give me five minutes and *don't move.*'

She spotted him between the swirling snow, just a dark shape lying prone, and the worst-case scenarios she had tussled with as she had flung on her jumper and scarf and coat and everything else smashed into her with the force of a ten-ton block of granite. What if he had suffered concussion? He would be able to sound coherent, make sense, only to die without warning. That had happened to someone, somewhere. She had read it in the news years ago. What if he had broken something? His spine? Fractured his leg or his arm? There was no way that a doctor would be able to get out here. Even a helicopter would have trouble in these weather conditions.

'Don't move!' She had brought two tablecloths with her. 'You can use these to cover yourself with and I'm going to get that table thing Dad uses for wallpapering. It can be rigged up like a stretcher.'

'Don't be so melodramatic, Jen. I just need you to help me up. The snow's so soft that it's impossible. I seem to have pulled a muscle in my back.'

'What if it's more serious than that, James?' she cried, kneeling and peering at him at close range. She shone her torch directly at his face and he winced away from the light.

'Would you mind directing the beam somewhere else?'

She ignored him. 'What I'm saying is that you shouldn't move if you think you might have done something to your spine. It's one of the first things you learn on a first-aid course.'

'You've done a first-aid course?'

'No, but I'm making an educated guess. Your colour looks good. That's a brilliant sign. How many fingers am I holding up?'

'What?'

'My fingers. How many of them am I holding up? I need to make sure that you aren't suffering from concussion...'

'Three fingers and move the bloody torch, Jennifer. Let me sling my arm around your neck and we're going to have to hobble to the cottage. I don't think I can make it all the way back to the house.'

'I'm not sure...'

'Okay, here's the deal. While you debate the shoulds and shouldn'ts, I'm going to pass out with hypothermia. I've pulled a muscle! I don't need the blankets and a make-shift stretcher, although I'm very grateful for the sugges-tion. I just need a helping hand.'

'Your voice sounds strong. Another good sign.'

'Jennifer!'

'Okay, but *I'm still not sure...*'

'I can live with that.'

He slung his arm around her neck and she felt the heavy, muscled weight of him as he levered himself up, with her help. The snow was thick and their feet sank into its depth, making it very difficult to balance and walk. It was little wonder that he hadn't been able to prise himself up. Even with her help, she could tell that he was in pain, unable to stand erect, his hand pressed to the base of his back.

They struggled back to the cottage. She had draped the tablecloths around him, even though he had done his best to resist and the torch cast a wavering light directly ahead, illuminating the snow and turning the spectral scenery into a winter wonderland.

'I could try and get hold of an ambulance service…' she suggested, out of breath because even though he was obviously doing his best to spare her his full weight, he was still six feet three inches of packed muscle.

'I never knew you were such a worrier.'

'What do you expect?' she demanded hotly. 'You were supposed to stroll over for dinner…'

'Didn't I tell you that it's impossible to stroll in snow this deep?'

'Stop trying to be funny! You were supposed to come to the cottage for dinner and the next time I hear from you, you're calling to tell me that you decided to chop down a tree and you're lying on the ground with a possible broken back!'

'I'm sorry if I worried you…'

'Yes,' Jennifer muttered, still angry with him for having sent her into a panic, still deathly worried that he was putting on a brave face because that was just the sort of man he was, 'well, you *should* be.'

'Have you cooked something delicious?'

'You shouldn't talk. You should conserve your energy.'

'Is that something else you picked up on the first-aid course you never went to?'

She felt her lips twitch and suppressed a desire to laugh. She got the feeling that he was doing his utmost to distract her from her worry, even though he would have been in a lot of discomfort and surely worried about himself. That simple generosity of spirit brought a lump of emotion to her throat and she stopped talking, for fear of bursting into tears.

Ahead of them the well-lit cottage beckoned like a port in a storm.

'Here at last.' She nudged open the door and deposited him on the sofa in the sitting room, where he collapsed with a groan.

He didn't have a broken spine. Nor was anything fractured. That much she had figured out on the walk back. He had pulled a muscle. Painful but not terminal.

She stood back, arms folded, and looked at him with jaundiced eyes.

'Now, admit it, James. It was very silly of you to think you could sort out that tree, wasn't it?'

'I managed to do what needed doing,' he countered. 'I fought the tree and the tree lost. The pulled muscle in my back is just collateral damage.'

Jennifer snorted in response. 'You'll have to get out of those clothes. They're soaking wet. I'm going to bring down some of Dad's. They won't be a terrific fit, but you'll have to work with it. Tomorrow I'll fetch some from your house.' She was resigned to the fact that they would now be stranded together, under the same roof.

James, eyes closed, grunted.

'But first, I'll go get you some painkillers. Dad keeps them in bulk supply for a rainy day. Or an emergency like this.'

'I don't do painkillers.'

'Too bad.'

Her father was shorter than James and thinner. She had no idea how his clothes would stretch to accommodate James's more muscular frame, but she chose the biggest of the tee shirts, a jumper and a pair of jogging bottoms with an elasticated waist, which were a five-year-old leg-acy from her father's days when he had decided to join the local gym, which he had tried once only to declare that gyms were for idiots who should be out and about.

'Clothes,' she announced, back in the sitting room, where the open fire kept the room beautifully warm. 'And first, painkillers.' She handed him two tablets with a glass of water and watched as he reluctantly swallowed them.

'You make a very good matron.' He handed her the glass of water and sighed as he began to defrost.

He grinned but she didn't find it very amusing. He had been a complete fool. He had, as was his nature, been so supremely confident of his strength that it would never have occurred to him that sorting out a tree in driving snow might have been an impossible mission. He had wor-ried her sick. And beyond both those things, she was stu-pidly annoyed to be compared to a *matron*. She privately and illogically rebelled against being the friend upon whom he could rely in a situation like this, the girl who wouldn't baulk in a crisis and was used to the harsh east-erly conditions, the tall, well-built girl who could tackle any physical situation with the best of them. She wanted to be seen as delicate and fragile and in need of manly pro-tection, and then she was annoyed with herself for being pathetic. Old feelings that she thought she had left behind seemed to be waiting round every corner, eager to ambush the person she had become.

'I'll leave you to get into some fresh clothes,' she said shortly. 'And I'll go and prepare us something to eat.'

She turned to walk away and he reached out to catch her hand and tug her to face him.

'In case you think I'm not grateful for your help, I am,' he said softly.

Jennifer didn't say anything because he was absentmindedly rubbing his thumb on the underside of her wrist, and for the first time since she had been flung into his company she had no resources with which to fight the stirrings of desire she had been trying so hard to subdue. She could barely breathe.

'I don't know what I would have done if you hadn't been here.'

'That's all right,' Jennifer croaked, then cleared her throat, while she wondered whether to snatch her hand out of his gently, delicately, caressing grasp.

'I know you weren't expecting to find me here when you arrived but I'm glad I was. I've missed you.'

She wanted to shout at him that he shouldn't use words like that, which made her fevered irrational brain start thinking all sorts of inappropriate things.

'Have you missed *me* or was I replaced by your hectic life and new-found independence?'

'I…I don't know what you expect me to say to that, James…' But she wondered whether this was his way of reasserting the balance between them, putting it back to that place where he could be certain that he knew where she stood, a place where the power balance was restored.

'Of course—' she pulled her hand away from him and took a step back '—I thought about you now and again and hoped that you were doing well. I meant to email you lots more than I actually did and I'm sorry about that…'

He looked at her in unreadable silence, which she was the first to break.

'I'll leave you to change.'

'I think it would probably be a good idea if I were to dry off a bit. It won't take long, but it'll be easier to get these clothes off if they aren't damp.'

'Makes sense.' Her nerves were still all over the place

and those fabulous midnight-blue eyes roving over her flushed face felt as intimate as his thumb had on her wrist.

'You've just come from outside. Sit for a while and get dry before you think of cooking.'

'Well…maybe just for a few minutes…' She sat on the chair closest to the fire and nervously looked at him. She had thought he hadn't changed at all in the past four years but he had. There was a tough maturity about him that hadn't yet crystallised when she had last seen him. His rise in the world of business had been meteoric. She knew that because, just once, she had given in to temptation and devoured everything she could about him on the Internet. She had discovered that he no longer limited himself to the company he had inherited, he had used that as a springboard for taking over failing companies and had gained a reputation for turning them around in record time. And yet, he had continued to resist the lure of marriage. Why? Was he so consumed by work that women were just satellites hovering on the periphery? Or did he just still enjoy playing the field which, as an eligible, staggeringly rich, good-looking bachelor, would have been a really huge field?

She felt the urge to burst through her self-imposed barrier and ask him and stifled it. She remembered the last time she had misread a situation.

'You've grown up,' he said so softly that she had to strain forward to hear him. 'You've lost that open, transparent way you used to have.'

'People *do* grow up,' she said abruptly.

'Were you hurt by that guy? That's the question I've been asking myself.'

For a few seconds, Jennifer didn't follow where he was going and then she realised that he was talking about Patric.

'He's my best friend!'

'Not sure that says anything.' James slanted her a look that made her go red. 'Were you in love with him? Did he break your heart? Because you seem a lot more cynical than you did four years ago. Sure, people change and grow up, but you're much more guarded now than you were then.'

Jennifer was lost for words. His take on her was revealing. He might have known, years ago, that she had a crush on him, but he obviously had never suspected the depth of her feelings. *She* had not really suspected the depth of her own feelings! It was only as she began dating that she realised how affected she had been by James's rejection, how deep her feelings for him ran. And returning here... all those feelings were making themselves felt once again.

The last thing she needed was him trying to get into her head!

'I love Patric,' she told him tightly. 'And I don't want to be psychoanalysed by you. I know you're probably bored, lying there unable to do anything, but I can bring you your computer and you can work.' The devil worked on idle hands and right now James was very idle.

'My computer's back at my house,' he said irritably, 'and I won't have you braving the snow to get it. I've done enough work for the day, anyway. I can afford to take a little time off.'

'Your mother would be pleased to hear that. She thinks you work too hard.'

'I thought you never talked about me with my mother.'

Jennifer shook her head when he grinned at her and stood up. 'I'm going to go and fix us something to eat. Get changed when you feel your clothes are dry enough.'

'What's on the menu?'

'Whatever appears on the plate in front of you.' She left

to the sound of his rich chuckle and she sternly stifled the temptation to laugh as well.

Her head was full of him as she went about the business of turning a bottle of crushed tomatoes, some cream and some mushrooms into something halfway decent to have with some of the tagliatelle her father kept in abundant supply in the larder. James annoyed her and alarmed her the way no one else had ever been able to, but he also made her laugh when she didn't want to and held her spellbound when she knew she shouldn't be. So what did that say about the state of her defences? She had thought that by seeing him again, she would have finally discovered that his impact had been diminished. She had foolishly imagined that she would put her demons to rest. The very opposite had happened, and, although she hated the thought of that, she was practically humming under her breath as she prepared their meal.

When she thought about him lying on the sofa in the sitting room, a wonderful, excited and *thoroughly forbidden* heat began spreading through her and she couldn't stop herself from liking it.

She took him his food on a tray and he waved her help aside as he struggled into a sitting position.

'The painkillers are kicking in.' He took a mouthful of food and then wondered where the wine was. Oh, and while she was about it, perhaps she could bring him some water as well.

Halfway through the meal, about which he was elaborately complimentary, he announced that he was now completely dry. He magnanimously informed her that there would be no need to wash his clothes, even though she hadn't offered.

'I have more than enough at home to get me through an enforced stay,' he decided, and Jennifer frowned at him.

'How long are you planning on staying?' she asked, not bothering to hide the sarcasm, and then she looked at him narrowly when he shrugged and smiled.

'How long is a piece of string?'

'That's no kind of answer, James.'

'Well, weather wise, even if the snow stops in the next five minutes, which is highly unlikely, we won't be leaving here for another couple of days. We both know that this is the last port of call for the snow ploughs. It's too deep for either of us to drive through and, in my condition, I can't do much about clearing it. That said, I don't think it's going to abate for at least another twenty-four hours, anyway. Longer if the weather forecast is to be believed.'

'Well, you're certainly the voice of doom,' Jennifer said, removing his tray from him, putting it on top of hers and sitting back down because she was, frankly, exhausted, despite having had a very lazy day, all things considered.

'I prefer to call it the voice of reality. Which brings me to point two. I can't go back to my house. I'm going to need help getting back on my feet. I'm putting on a brave front, but I can barely move.' She hadn't exactly been the most welcoming of friends when she had discovered him in the cottage, but, hell, however hard she fought it, there was still something there between them. Friendship, attraction…he didn't know. He just knew that the frisson between them did something for him. As did looking at her. As did hearing her laugh and seeing her smile and catching her slipping him sidelong looks when she didn't think his attention was on her. He relished this enforced stay and, while his back was certainly not in a particularly good way, he silently thanked it for giving him the opportunity to get to the bottom of her.

Jennifer was torn as to whether to believe him or not. On the one hand, he had always claimed to have the constitution of an ox. He was known to boast that he never fell prey to viruses and that his only contact with a doctor had been on the day of his birth. He surely wouldn't lie when it came to admitting pain.

On the other hand, he didn't look in the slightest regretful about his circumstances. In fact, for someone in the grip of back pain, he seemed remarkably breezy.

Breezy or not, she couldn't send him hobbling back to his house although the thought of him in the cottage with her made her stomach tighten into knots of apprehension. Four years of hiding had been rewarded with such a concentrated dose of him that she was struggling to maintain the fiction that the effect he had on her was history. It wasn't. Anything but.

'So…as it stands, I'm going to have to fetch clothes for you for an enforced stay of indefinite duration, plus your laptop…plus I'm going to have to feed and water you…'

'There's no need to sound so thrilled at the prospect…'

'This just isn't what I banked on when I began this journey to the cottage.'

'No,' James said drily, 'because you didn't even expect to find me here.'

'But I'm glad I did,' she told him with grudging truthfulness. 'Four years is a long time. I was in danger of forgetting what you looked like.'

'And have I lived up to expectation?'

'You look older than you are,' Jennifer said snidely, because his ego was already big enough as it was.

'That's very kind of you.' But he grinned. That boyish, sexy grin that had always been able to set her pulses racing. 'Now you're going to have to do me yet another favour, I'm afraid.'

'You want coffee. Or tea. Or something else to drink. And you'd like something sweet to finish off the meal.

Maybe a home-made dessert of some kind. Am I along the right lines?'

'Could I trust you to make me a home-made dessert?' he asked lazily. 'Don't forget that my knowledge of your love of cooking goes back a long way…' He held her eyes and Jennifer, skewered by the intensity of his gaze, half opened her mouth to say something and discovered that she had forgotten what she had been about to say. Colour slowly crawled into her face and, to break the suffocating tension, she stood up to get the two plates and carry them into the kitchen.

'So tea or coffee, then,' she said briskly. 'Which is it to be? Dad has a million varieties of tea you could choose from. The larder seems to have had a massive overhaul ever since he decided to take up cooking. Apparently one brand of tea is no longer good enough.'

'I need you to help me undress.'

'I beg your pardon?'

'I can't manoeuvre to get the trousers off, even though the painkillers are beginning to kick in.'

Jennifer froze. For a few seconds all her vital functions seemed to shut down. When they re-engaged, she knew that, in the name of this friendship that they were tentatively rebuilding, she should think nothing of providing the help he needed. He had no qualms asking for it. He wasn't going into meltdown at the thought of her touching him. She had loftily told him that he should see her as a friend rather than a woman, so what was he going to think if, *as a friend*, she told him that she couldn't possibly…?

'Have you tried?'

'I don't need to try. Every time I make the smallest movement, my back protests.'

Jennifer took a deep breath and walked towards him. What choice did she have?

James slung his arm over her shoulders, felt the softness of her skin underneath the jumper she was wearing, breathed in her clean fresh scent, the smell of the cold outdoors still lingering on her skin.

'Well, thank goodness I'm not one of these five-foot-nothing girls you go out with,' she managed to joke, although her vocal cords felt unnaturally dry and strained. 'You would still be lying in the snow outside or else dragging yourself back to the house the best you could.'

'Why do you make fun of yourself?'

'I don't.' She helped him into a sitting position. His skin was clammy. Underneath the breezy façade, he was obviously in a great deal of discomfort, yet he had not taken it out on her. While she had been reluctantly catering to his demands and not bothering to hide the fact that she wasn't overjoyed at having him under her roof, he had been suffering in silence. Shame and guilt washed over her.

'You do. You've always done it.' He had unbuttoned his shirt and he grimaced as she eased him out of it, down to the white tee shirt underneath. 'I remember when you were sixteen laughing at yourself, telling me about the outfits your friends were wearing to go out, making fun of your height and—'

'I can't concentrate when you're talking!' She was red-faced and flustered because those were memories she didn't want thrown at her.

'You're a sexy woman,' he said roughly.

'I'll help you to your feet so that we can get the trousers off.' He thought *she was a sexy woman*. Why did he have to say that? Why did he have to open a door in her head through which all sorts of unwanted thoughts could find their way in? He hadn't thought she was *a sexy woman* four years ago, she reminded herself fiercely. Oh, no! Four years ago he had shoved her away!

She didn't have to look at him as she began easing the trousers off. On their downward path, she was aware of black tight-fitting underwear, the length and strength of his legs, his muscled calves. She was in danger of passing out, and even more so when she heard his voice in her head telling her that she was a sexy woman.

Patric had never made her feel this way when he had told her that she was sexy. Hearing Patric tell her that she was sexy had made her want to giggle uncontrollably.

'This is crazy,' she said in a muffled voice, her face bright red as she sprang back to her feet and snatched the jogging bottoms she had earlier brought down.

'Why is it crazy?'

'Because you…you need a professional to help you. A qualified nurse! What if I do something wrong and you… you damage yourself?' She was mesmerised by the sight of his legs, the dark hair on them, the rock hardness of his calves. She didn't dare allow her eyes to travel farther up. Instead, she focused furiously on the jogging bottoms and his feet as he stepped into them, supporting himself by his hand on her shoulder.

'I thought you already gave me all the vital checks?'

'Not funny, James! There. Done!'

'Tee shirt. Might as well get rid of that as well.' He slowly sank back down on the sofa.

Jennifer wondered whether this would ever end. He thought she was *sexy*. What did he feel as her fingers made contact with his skin? Did it do anything for him, considering he thought that she was *a sexy woman*? She fought back the tide of inappropriate questions ricocheting in her head and pulled his tee shirt off, where it joined the rest of his now barely damp clothes on the ground, and helped him with the tee shirt she had grabbed from her father's chest of drawers.

None of the clothes fitted him properly. The jogging bottoms were too short and the tee shirt was too tight. He should have looked ridiculous but he didn't. He just carried on looking sinfully, unfairly, disturbingly sexy.

'Okay. I'm going to stick these in the wash and have a shower and then I'll make you some coffee. I'm sure Dad has some sleeping tablets somewhere in his bedroom from when he did his back in a few years ago. Shall I get them for you?'

'Painkillers are about as far as I'm prepared to go when it comes to taking tablets.'

Jennifer shrugged and backed towards the door, clutching the clothes in one hand like a talisman.

Anyone would imagine, he thought with sudden irritation, that she had been asked to walk on a bed of hot coals. She made lots of noises about friendship but her body language was telling a different story. This wasn't the girl upon whom he had always thought he could rely. This wasn't the girl fascinated by his stories and willing to go the extra mile for him. This was a woman inconvenienced by his presence, a woman determined to keep him at a distance. He had hurt her once and she had moved on, leaving him behind in her wake. The knowledge was frustrating. He wondered how well he had ever known her. She had skimmed over her relationship with the Frenchman and had mentioned no other guys, although he was sure that there would have been some. The woman was a knockout. But whereas once she would have happily confided in him, leaving no detail out, this was no longer the case. He could remember a time when she had laughed and told him little stories about the people she went to school with and, later, to university. No more.

Fair's fair, he thought. Did she know *him*? He was uneasily aware that a relationship flowed two ways. It was something he was poorly equipped for. His relationships with women were disposable and had always involved more effort on their part than on his.

James was not given to this level of pointless introspection and he pushed it aside.

'Well, it's up to you,' she was saying now with a dismissive shrug. 'I think, as well, that you should sleep down here. The sofa is big enough and comfortable enough and it'll save you the trip up the stairs. There's a downstairs toilet, as you know…I know the bath is upstairs but I'm sure you'll be able to manage things better…tomorrow…after you've had a good night's sleep…' She hoped so because she drew the line at helping him into a bath or under the shower. Just thinking about it made her feel a little wobbly.

Having delivered that speech in a surprisingly calm, controlled, neutral voice, she fled up the stairs, had a very quick shower, which was blissful, and then returned to the sitting room with an armful of bed linen. She had expected to find him still lying on the sofa but he wasn't. He had moved to one of the chairs and switched the television on. Wall-to-wall coverage of the weather.

Quickly and efficiently, she began making up the sofa with two sheets, the duvet which she had pilfered from her father's bed, likewise the pillows.

'You probably shouldn't be taxing your back too much,' she said, hovering by the sofa because she didn't intend to stay down and watch television with him. There was danger in this pretend domesticity and she had no intention of falling prey to it.

'The more I tax it, the faster I'll be back on my feet,' James said curtly, realising, from her dithering, that she had no intention of being in his company any more than was strictly necessary. Her body language was telling him that, whatever common ground they had managed to carve out for themselves, she still hadn't signed up to be stuck with him in the cottage for an indefinite period of time. That was beyond the call of duty.

'Aren't you going to relax and watch some television with me?' he asked, perversely drawn to hearing her confirm what was going through his head, and his mouth twisted cynically as she shook her head and stammered out some excuse about still having to clear the kitchen, being really tired after the day's events, needing to finish some emails she had started earlier in the afternoon…

'In that case,' he said coolly, 'I wouldn't dream of keeping you. If you make sure that the painkillers are at hand, then I'll see you in the morning.' He stood up, waved aside her offer of assistance and made his way back to the sofa, where he lay down carefully as she left the sitting room, closing the door quietly behind her.

CHAPTER FOUR

IT DIDN'T take long for Jennifer to work out that James made a very demanding patient.

She awoke the following morning at seven-thirty and tiptoed downstairs to discover that the light in the sitting room was on, as was the television, which was booming out the news. James was on the sofa and she stood for a moment in the doorway to the sitting room with her dressing gown wrapped tightly around her, drinking him in. She had hoped to simply grab a cup of coffee and retreat back to her bedroom for a another hour's worth of sleep, but he noticed her and glanced across broodingly at her silhouette.

'There's no end to this snow,' were his opening words. The curtains had been pulled open as if to reinforce his darkest suspicion that they were, indeed, still stranded in a sea of white. 'The last time it snowed like this, life didn't return to normal for two weeks. I have work to do.'

'That goes for the both of us,' Jennifer muttered, ungluing herself from the doorway and stepping into the sitting room to toss a few logs into the now-dead fire.

She had exhausted herself wondering how she was going to deal with James under her roof. She had feverishly analysed the heady, unhealthy mix of emotions his presence generated, had shakenly viewed her loss of calm as a dangerous and possibly slippery slope to a place she couldn't even begin to imagine, a place where she once again became captive to feelings she had spent years stuffing away out of sight. Now she realised that, while she had been consumed with her own emotional turmoil, he likewise was counting down to when they could part company.

She sourly wondered if *making the best of things* was becoming a strain. Add to that the fact that he was now out of action and she could understand why he was contemplating the still-falling snow with an expression of loathing.

'I've had to let Paris know that I can't say when I'll be back. I'm missing Patric's next exhibition, which I had been looking forward to. You're not the only one desperate to get out of here!'

James wondered whether she could make things any clearer. If she had had skis, he would not have been surprised to find her strapping them to her feet so that she could use them.

And who cared whether she happened to be missing her ex-boyfriend's exhibition? He thought back to the fair-haired man with the earring and the fedora and scowled. They had gone out and broken up. Who, in God's name, remained good friends with their ex-partner? It was unhealthy. His mood, which had been grim the night before when she had made it clear that the last thing she wanted was his company, became grimmer in receipt of this unwanted piece of information.

'I've been up since five,' James told her, levering himself into a sitting position.

'Wasn't the sofa comfortable?'

'It's big but so am I. I wouldn't say it's been the most amazing night's sleep. My back was in agony.'

'I left some painkillers...'

By way of response, James held up the plastic tub and tipped it upside down. 'Not enough and I didn't have the energy to hobble into the kitchen to see if I could find more. Your father has an eccentric way of storing things.'

Jennifer, ashamed because she had spared little thought for his back in between her own inner confusion, instantly told him to wait right there, that she would get him some painkillers immediately, something stronger than paracetamol.

'Where am I supposed to go?' James asked sarcastically. 'I am literally at your mercy.'

Jennifer almost grinned. He was always so masterful, so much in control, the guy who was never fazed by anything and yet here he was now as sullen and as sulky as a child deprived of his Christmas treat because the body on which he depended had let him down.

'I like the sound of that,' she told him and he quirked an eyebrow and then reluctantly smiled.

'Really? So what do you intend to do with me?'

Jennifer didn't know whether there was any kind of double meaning to that soft drawl, but she felt the hairs on the back of her neck stand on end.

'Well...' be brisk and keep it all on an impersonal level, two friends thrown together against their will, two friends who had absolutely no history '...first of all I shall go and get you some painkillers. A full tub of them, although I don't have to tell you that under no circumstances are you to go over the allotted dosage—'

'There's a career in nursing crying out for you—'

'And then—' she ignored his interruption '—I shall light that fire because this room is pretty cold—'

'Fire went out some time around two in the morning.'

'You were up at two in the morning?'

'Between the sudden drop in temperature and the agony in my back, sleep was difficult.'

Jennifer, distracted from her list of things to do, wasn't sure whether to believe him or not. The advantage to their familiarity with one another was that there was no need to continually try and be entertaining or even talkative. The disadvantage was that he would see no need whatsoever to be on his best behaviour.

'And then I shall go up to your house and fetch whatever it is you want me to fetch.'

She didn't give him time to ask any questions. Instead, she went to the kitchen, located a box of strong painkillers and took them in with a glass of water.

'You'll have to help me into a sitting position.'

'Honestly, James, stop milking it.' But she helped him up and she knew, although she could barely admit it to herself, that she liked the feel of his body. She could tell herself that she had to be careful until the cows came home, but it was heady and treacherously thrilling to touch him, even if the touching, like this, was completely innocent.

Flustered, she turned her attention to the dead fire, and she began going through the routine of relighting it. It was something she had done a million times. More logs would have to be brought in from the shed outside. She hoped that they would have been cut. Her father was reliable when it came to making sure that they were well stocked over the winter months. Snow, at some point, was inevitable and it never paid to take something as simple as electricity for granted. Too many times it had failed, leaving them without heating.

James edged himself up a bit more and watched, fascinated, as she dealt expertly with the fire. He had turned down the volume on the television when she had entered the sitting room and the flickering light from the TV picked out the shine in her long, wavy hair, which fell across her face as she knelt in front of the fireplace.

She wasn't one of those useless, helpless women who thought that their role in life was to be dependent. Her slender hands efficiently did what had to be done. Her robe had fallen open and he could see her tee shirt underneath and the shorts that she slept in. Sensible sleeping wear and never, he thought, had he ever seen anything so damned sexy.

James was taken aback by the sudden ferocity of his arousal and he realised that it had been there from the start, practically from the moment he had laid eyes on her again. He whipped the duvet over him because she wouldn't have been able to miss the definition of his erection underneath the jogging bottoms that she had brought down for him the evening before and that he was still wearing.

His breath caught in his throat when, eventually, she stood up, all five foot leggy ten, and brushed her hands together to shake off some of the woody dust and ash. She had forgotten that she was supposed to clutch the dressing gown around her and now he had an eyeful of long, shapely legs and the brevity of a tee shirt that delineated full, firm breasts. He thought back to four years previously when she had offered herself to him, thought back to how close he had come to taking what had been on offer, only pulling back because he had known, instinctively, that a vulnerable girl with little experience didn't need a man like him. Desire for her now slammed into him and he half closed his eyes.

'No wonder you have to pull that duvet over you.' Jennifer walked towards him and James looked at her. She was resting her hands on her waist and wore a reproving expression. 'It's cold in here even with the heating on. You should have yelled for me to come down and light the fire. I would have understood that you couldn't do it yourself.'

James shifted and dragged his eyes away from those abundant orbs barely contained underneath the skimpy tee shirt. In resting her hands on her waist, she had pushed aside the dressing gown and was it his imagination or could he see, in the grey, indistinct light, the outline of her nipples?

'I was hardly about to do that when you made it clear that taking care of me for five minutes was a chore,' he said gruffly, dragging his eyes away from the alluring sight.

Jennifer flushed guiltily in the face of this blunt accusation. He couldn't even look her in the face and she could understand why. She had been a miserable friend, taking out her insecurities on him when he had done nothing but try and fix the gaping hole four years of absence had left in their friendship. In return, she had sniped, chastised and been grudging in her charity. God, he was probably close to truly disliking her.

When she thought about that, about him really not wanting to spend time in her company, she was filled with a sour, sickening anguish.

Although she had been at pains to avoid him for four long years, she had never, actually, thought about the simple truth, which was that she had engineered the destruction of a long-standing friendship. She had thought that the choice was a simple one. All or nothing. And in Paris she had managed to kid herself that nothing was achievable. It wasn't. Her heart picked up speed and she longed for him to look at her again instead of averting his eyes from her the way he would have averted them from a stranger who couldn't be bothered to help out in a crisis.

'I'm sorry if that was the impression I gave you, James. I didn't mean to. It's not a chore. Of course, it isn't.'

'You've made it perfectly clear that this is the last place on the face of the earth you want to be, especially when there's the exciting pull of Paris, parties and important exhibitions to view.'

'I never said anything about parties,' Jennifer mumbled. Disconcertingly, the exhibition that she had been looking forward to when she had left Paris now held little appeal. Technicolor reality was happening right here and everything else had been reduced to an out-of-focus, inconsequential background blur.

'And Patric will be fine hosting his exhibition without me. In fact, sometimes those things can be a little bit tiring.'

James, who couldn't think of the blond man without feeling distinctly uptight, pricked up his ears. He looked as she perched on the side of the sofa and picked absently at the tassel on one of the cushions, which she had rescued from the ground where it had landed at some point during the night.

'Really?' he asked in an encouraging voice and she shot him a guilty look from under her lashes.

James kept his eyes firmly fixed on her face because anywhere else would have been disastrous for the array of responses his body was having in her presence. Those were definitely her nipples outlined against the soft cotton tee shirt. He could see the tips of them. It was just one reason to make sure he looked directly at her face, although even that made him feel a little giddy.

'I love art and I just love going to exhibitions and, of course, I would do anything in the world to help Patric out, but sometimes it gets a little boring at those dos. Lots of glamorous people trying to outdo one another. The women are always dripping with jewellery and most of the men barely look at the paintings because they are into investment art. You see, Patric's parents are rather well connected so the guest list is usually…well…full of the Great and the Good…'

'Sounds tedious,' James murmured. 'Can't stand that kind of thing myself…'

'It *can* be a little dull,' Jennifer confided. 'But the financial climate is tough out there and art is a luxury buy at the end of the day. Patric has no option but to put up with stuff like that.'

'Maybe he enjoys it…' James was keen to insinuate that the wonderful best-buddy-confidante thing might have been something of an illusion. People who go abroad could be very susceptible to the kindness of strangers. 'He certainly looked on top of the world in those pictures I saw of him. Big grin, lots of hot babes around him…'

'He always has a lot of hot babes around him.' Jennifer laughed. 'He's that kind of person. Women are attracted to him. He doesn't try to hide his feminine side.'

'You're telling me that the man's gay?'

'I'm telling you no such thing!' But she found herself laughing, right back in that place where they had always been so good together. 'He's just in tune with women, likes talking about the things they like talking about, and he's also a massive flirt.'

James wanted to ask her if that was why they had broken up. Had she, perhaps, caught him in bed with one of those hot babes to whom he had been pouring out his heart, showing his sensitive side, while simultaneously chatting about clothes and shoes and feelings?

But regrettably she was standing up and telling him that she would go and get changed and get the day started.

'I'll bring you some breakfast,' she said, 'just as soon as I've had a shower. Er…' Should she ask him whether he wanted a shower? A bath, maybe, if he was up to that?

She decided not to because just the thought of helping him get undressed made her feel light-headed and horribly, horribly turned on.

'Er…I won't be long…' She thought about helping him get naked, wondered what he would look like and felt faint at the thought of it. 'You can make a list of what you want me to bring back from the house for you and I'll need your key. I know Dad has one but I have a feeling he keeps it on his key ring, which he took with him to Scotland.'

For the first time since she had arrived at the cottage and run slap bang into James, Jennifer was feeling on top of the world as she quickly showered and changed into a pair of faded jeans, a vest, a tee shirt, a jumper and some very thick knee-high socks. She knew why. Keeping him at a continual distance was hard work. Of course, she wasn't about to start being overly chummy, giggling and forgetting that he was the guy who had broken her young heart, but it was just a hell of a lot easier to let him in just a little.

At any rate she had no choice, did she? He was laid up, unable to move. She *had* to physically help him! If she could open up and be friends with him once more, it would just prove that she had got over him! More or less! Those niggly, confused, tumultuous, excited feelings she was having would therefore be nothing to worry about!

The list was ready when she returned. On it he had written, 'laptop, charger, clothes'.

'But before you disappear,' he said, making it sound as though she were Scott of the Antarctic, 'I'm feeling a little peckish…'

She was still feeling strangely upbeat when, forty-five minutes later, she headed off to his house. The estate was so vast that no other dwelling could be glimpsed from any window in the house. In summer, the trees shielded the view of the house but those trees now were bare and heavy with snow and it was a battle against the wind and the snow to make it to the front door. She had been to the house before but never to his bedroom, which she managed to locate by a process of elimination. The top of the house was comprised of a suite of rooms, and was virtually closed off, used only for guests. Of the other bedrooms, only one, apart from Daisy's, resembled a room that was occupied.

Deep burgundy floor-length drapes were pulled open so that she could see, outside, the steady swirl of the never-ending snow. Most of the pale carpet was covered by a sprawling Persian rug and a massive four-poster bed dominated much of the room. It was neatly made up but, when she leaned against the doorframe and closed her eyes, she could picture James lying on it, wickedly, sensationally sexy, with dark satin sheets lightly covering his bronzed muscular body. Then she pictured him on that sofa, with the duvet over him as she perched on the edge and chatted to him, so close that their bodies had been practically touching. She blinked guiltily and the image was gone.

Locating a handful of clothes took no time at all but it felt uncomfortable gathering them up, jumpers, trousers, tee shirts and underwear. Designer items neatly laundered and tossed into the drawer indiscriminately. She had grabbed two plastic bags before leaving the cottage and she stuffed all the items inside and then hunted down his laptop computer and charger, both of which were in the kitchen where he had left them before his heroic mission to fell the tree.

She had left him lying on the sofa and he was still there when she finally returned, although he had decided that he couldn't remain prone for ever.

'I can manage to move a bit when the painkillers kick in,' he announced, liking the way the wet made the waves in her long hair turn into curls. Her dark hair was dramatic against the paleness of her skin and he didn't think he had ever noticed before how long her lashes were or how satiny smooth her complexion.

'But I don't think it's going to do any good if I try and work sitting up on the sofa,' he pushed himself up, flexed his muscles and grimaced when his back made itself felt. 'I should be upright. You'd probably know that if you'd done that first-aid course you never got around to doing.'

'So what are you suggesting?' Jennifer asked drily.

'Well…I can use that chair over there but you might have to bring me some sort of desk. We can position it by the bay window.'

'What sort of desk did you have in mind, sir?'

'Would it be asking too much for you to get the one I use at the house? It's roughly eight by four.' He grinned and felt a kick when she grinned back at him and shook her head with an elaborate sigh.

'I suppose I could bring down my dressing table. It's small and light and it'll have to do.' She glanced down at the clothes she had brought over in the plastic bag. 'Can you manage to change yourself?'

'Only after I've had a shower, but I figure I can just about make it up the stairs myself. If you could lend me a towel…'

She did and while he showered—she could hear the water and could picture him standing under it—she cleared the little dressing table and manoeuvred it down the stairs where she set up a miniature work station for him. An office away from his office with a view of the snowy landscape.

The cottage was small and, having avoided him the night before, leaving him to watch television on his own, she resigned herself to the fact that she wasn't similarly going to be able to avoid him during daylight hours. She could work in the kitchen and she would, but even stretching her legs would entail walking into the sitting room.

Far from feeling discomforted by the prospect of that, as she had the evening before, she felt as if something had changed between them. Despite her best efforts, she had stopped fighting herself and relaxed.

He had forgone the hassle of shaving and he emerged half an hour later with wet hair and just enough of a stubble so that he looked even darker and sexier. Reluctantly she was forced to admit that neither Patric nor Gerard, the erstwhile lawyer with whom she had tried to forge a relationship, were a patch on James when it came to sheer animal sex appeal.

He took himself off to the sitting room with a pot of coffee and Jennifer tried to concentrate on catching up with her emails in the kitchen. It was almost impossible. Eventually, she began reading some of her father's recipe books, amused when she noticed a number of pages creased, dishes he had either tried or else had put on a list to try at some stage.

In the midst of trying to decide whether she should just abandon all hope of concentrating on work and start cooking something a little more ambitious for their dinner, she was interrupted by the sound of a book hitting the ground with force and she yelped and jumped to her feet.

James was standing by the window with his hand pressed against the base of his back and scowling. He turned as she entered and greeted her with, 'Why do people resist doing something when they must know that it's for their own good!'

Jennifer looked down at the heavy book that had hit the floor. It was her father's gardening tome.

'Apologies. I had to throw something.'

'Do you throw something every time you get frustrated?' she asked, moving to collect the book and replace it on the little coffee table.

'My favoured way of releasing stress is to go to the gym and punch-bag it out of my system. Unfortunately that's impossible at the moment.' He felt a lot less stressed now that she was in the room. 'What are you doing in the kitchen? Are you working?'

'I'm reading a recipe book and wondering whether I should chance cooking something a little more ambitious a bit later. Shall I get you something to eat? Drink?'

'No, but you can sit and talk to me.' He gave up the chair in favour of the sofa and lay down with a sigh of intense relief.

'Your secretary must have a nightmarish time working for you,' Jennifer commented, moving to the comfy chair by the fire and tucking her legs under her.

She marvelled at how easy it was to slide back into this easy companionship and how much she was appreciating it, having feared it to be lost and gone for good. She tried not to think that it was no good for her and then decided that she was just, finally, dealing with things in an adult fashion. Not hiding, not fighting, just accepting and moving on. What could be dangerous or unhealthy about that? Besides, she enjoyed looking at him, even though she hated admitting that weakness to herself. She liked seeing him rake his fingers through his hair as he was doing now. It was a gesture that had followed him all through his teenage years.

'My secretary loves working for me,' he denied. 'She can't wait to start work in the mornings.'

Jennifer imagined someone young, pretty and adoring, following him with her eyes and working overtime just to remain in his company, and suddenly was sick with jealousy. 'She's in her sixties, a grandmother, with a retired husband who gets under her feet. Working for me is like having a permanent holiday.'

The relief that flooded her set up a series of alarm bells in her head and she resolutely ignored them. So that crush she had had might not have been quite as dead and buried as she had hoped, but she could deal with that!

He was grinning at her and she smiled back and said something about his ego, but teasingly, blushing when he continued to look at her with those fabulous deep blue eyes.

'So tell me why you threw the book,' she said, still feeling a little hot and bothered by his lingering stare. She knew that it wasn't good to feed an addiction, however much you thought you were in control, but she found she just couldn't stand up and walk back to the kitchen and carry on reading recipe books.

'A couple of months ago, we finalised a deal with a publishing company. On the whole a lucrative buyout with a lot of potential to go somewhere, but one of the subsidiary companies is having a problem toeing the line.'

Jennifer leaned forward, intrigued. She remembered reading about that buyout on the Internet. 'What do you mean *toeing the line*?'

'They need to amalgamate. They have a niche market but it makes no money. The employees could be absorbed into the mainstream publishing company and get on board with ebooks but they're making all sorts of uncooperative noises and refusing to sign on the dotted line without a fight. Of course, they could be made to toe the line but I'd rather not take on board disgruntled employees.'

Jennifer had worked with a couple of small publishing houses in Paris, one of which specialised in maps, the other in rare limited edition books. She had been fascinated to find how differently they were run from their mainstream brothers and how different the employees were. They were individually involved in their companies in a way ordinary employees tended not to be. Both had successfully broken away from the umbrella of the mother company and both were doing all right but hardly brilliantly. Without any security blanket, it was tough going.

She peppered him with questions about the legal standing of the company he was involved with, quite forgetting her boredom in the kitchen when she had been unable to concentrate on work.

Digging into her experiences with similar companies, she expanded on all the problems they had faced when they had successfully completed management buyouts.

'You want to work with them,' she said earnestly. 'You can exploit a different market. It doesn't all have to be about ebooks and online reads. I personally think it's worth having that niche market operating without interference because it really lends integrity to the bigger picture.'

James, who had had no real idea of what Jennifer did in Paris, had only known that whatever she did, she did extremely well, was impressed by the depth of her knowledge and the incisiveness of her ideas. She also knew all the legal ins and outs should this small arm of his publishing firm decide to break away. He found himself listening to her with interest and when, pink cheeked, she finally rounded up her rousing argument for not trying to force them to fit into a prescribed mould, he nodded slowly and frowned.

'Very good,' he said slowly, and she flushed with pleasure. 'So you think I should stop trying to close this minor arm of the business and let the employees do their own thing?'

'Not *do their own thing*,' Jennifer said, 'but with someone good in charge, you might be pleasantly surprised to find that there's room in this computerised world of ours to accommodate things that don't want to or can't be computerised. There are still people out there with a love of old things and we should encourage that.'

'And what would you say if I told you that I have just the person for that job in mind?'

'Have you? I guess I always thought that the people who work for you were bright young things who wouldn't want to get tied up with something they might see as old-fashioned.'

'Oh, some of the bright young things could be easily persuaded into tying themselves into something old-fashioned if the pay was right. Money is always the most effective arm twister.'

'Ye-es…' She dragged out that single syllable as she thought about what he said. 'But you also need someone who's really interested in what they're doing and not doing it just because the pay cheque at the end of the month is fat.'

'The person I have in mind is bright, passionate and would do a damn good job.'

'That's brilliant. Well…enough of me spouting my opinions. Do you feel a little less frustrated now or am I going to hear that gardening book hit the ground again? Not that I mind, but maybe you could give me a little advance warning so that I don't jump out of my skin when I happen to be holding a knife about to chop something up for our dinner!' She began standing up and he waved her back down.

'I like you spouting your opinions,' he said, which made her flush with pleasure again. 'The girl I knew just used to hang onto mine.'

And the guy I knew and with whom I was so infatuated never encouraged me to have my own...

The shift in their relationship now stared her in the face. Two adults finding ground that was equal, so different from what they once had, so different and *so much more rewarding.*

From nowhere floated those little words he had said when she had still been fighting him, still trying to prove to him how little he meant to her...

You're a sexy woman. Her heart skipped a beat and her skin began to tingle. He might respect her opinions, she thought, but that didn't mean that he had suddenly stopped seeing her as the girl next door. This time, when she tried to dredge up the hurt she felt she had suffered at his hands all those years ago, it eluded her. It was in the process of being replaced by something else. For the very first time, she thought back to that night and tried to see herself through his eyes. Young, naive, infatuated, gullible. What a poor proposition. She shook her head, clearing it of the muddle of thoughts now released to show themselves.

'I know. How boring for you.'

'Boring...never...'

'Who,' she said hurriedly, because that thoughtful look in his eyes was doing all sorts of weird things to her, 'do you have in mind for this job, then? And do you think he'll like being taken away from what he's doing to head up something that might not be a profitable concern?'

'It's a she...'

All at once Jennifer's overactive imagination, the very one she had tried to subdue, was back in play, throwing up images of a little blonde thing, cute and brainy, simpering and doing whatever was asked of her. One of his loyal employees, like his secretary only much younger and not married.

'The only fly in the ointment,' James said, watching her very carefully and marvelling at the fact that she still didn't seem to have a clue where this conversation was leading, 'is that she doesn't actually work for my company.'

'She doesn't?'

'Nope. In fact, she doesn't even work in the country.' He let those words pool in silence between them and smiled as it began to dawn on her that he was asking her to work for him.

'*I* can't work for you, James!'

'Why not? You said yourself that you were thinking of returning to England, that your father is getting older and will need you around more than he has done... Have you changed your mind about that?'

'No, but—'

'And this isn't a job offered to you out of charity. You talked yourself into it, as a matter of fact. Everything you said is spot on. It'll be the biggest challenge of your life and I guarantee you'll love every second of it.'

'Surely you have people within your company who are more qualified for the position.'

'None as passionate as you and certainly none with the required experience in dealing with a tiny, stubborn company that refuses to shift with the times.'

'I don't know what to say...'

'Then think about it.' He closed his eyes and listened to her soft breathing. 'Now what were you saying about that exciting meal you were going to prepare for me...?'

CHAPTER FIVE

'I NEVER said that it was going to be *exciting*…'

'And you'll give some consideration to my offer while you cook…'

'Are you sure you're being serious about this, James? You've never worked with me. I don't want you to get back to London and realise that you did the wrong thing because you weren't in your normal surroundings. I can't afford to jack my job in to discover that you've made a mistake.'

'I never make mistakes.'

'And you're never laid up, yet here you are. Laid up.'

'Do you ever do anything without putting up an argument?' But his slow smile addled her. 'I mean it. You'd be perfect for the job. You can join that little team and you can all argue together about the ills of capitalism and big conglomerates wiping out small concerns.'

'Is that what they've been saying to you?' She grinned, liking the sound of that team already.

'Something like that. I've never met a more stubborn bunch of people. They've been allowed to be fully self-accounting, thanks to their very woolly-headed, charming, eighty-two-year-old boss and, now that they face the threat of being held to account, they refuse to surrender. I think one of them may have said something along the lines of they'll go down fighting. None of them have realised that they've already been taken over and they don't have much choice but to get with the programme.'

'But you're not hard-hearted enough to force them.'

'Like I said, a disgruntled employee is worse than no employee at all.'

Her heart flipped over. James Rocchi might be powerful and ruthless, but he was also fair-minded and sympathetic. He was all those things she had always seen under the surface.

'And what about their eighty-two-year-old boss? Did they feel betrayed that he'd sold them out?'

'It wasn't a hostile takeover,' James said. 'Far from it. Edward Cable was a friend of my father's even though he was considerably older. He came to me for a rescue bid. One of the big publishing houses wanted them. They were a failing company but he was reluctant to sell out to someone who would pick them apart and throw aside the bits they didn't want without thought to the employees. I have next to no experience with publishing companies and no desire to add one to my stable but...'

'But you felt you had to do the decent thing.'

'Perhaps it was my sensitive, feminine side coming out...'

Jennifer wished he would stop doing that, making her laugh, making her see him as the three-dimensional man she had never glimpsed as a young girl.

'Edward was extremely grateful to me and I could afford to buy him out. In actual fact, like I said, the company has a lot of promise. There's enough there for them to carry that little wayward arm of their company which is what I suspect he's been doing all these years.'

'Then why the need to sell?'

'Because they were making less and less money and he's never had a family. No children to inherit. A family

business in a fast-moving world that doesn't have much
time for family businesses unless they're incredibly well
run with top-of-the-range IT departments that can take
them into the twenty-first century.'

'I'll think about it.' She stood up, flexed her legs and
headed out to the kitchen with a lot on her mind.

Should she take a job that would require her to work
for James? If that had been suggested when she had been
in Paris, hunkered down with him out of sight, she would
have run a mile from the idea, but out here, forced to
face him once again, she was discovering that he was not
the *bad guy* of her imagination. And the job sounded as
though it could be fun. In fact, it sounded like a job that
would be right up her street. Should she turn it down because it involved James? Should she let pride get in the
way of a good deal?

She prepared a meal on autopilot. They were now running out of fresh vegetables and, with the snow still falling
and no idea when she would next be seeing a shop, she made
do with tinned vegetables. Her father's larder was well
stocked. It was the sort of larder that would keep a small
family in food for weeks in the event of a nuclear fall-out.

She was busily opening a can when she heard James's
deep velvety voice at the door and she started and spun
round to see him lounging indolently against the doorframe. Immediately her body went into overdrive. How
was it that he was capable of dominating the space around
him so that it was impossible to remain detached?

'I've come to lend a hand.' He pushed himself away
from the door and sauntered into the kitchen to peer over
her shoulder. 'What feast are you preparing?'

'Nothing.'

He picked up the recipe book that she was following
in a half-hearted way and scrutinised it, reciting the in-

gredients and then checking them off on what he could spy on the counter.

Up close and personal, his presence next to her was making it impossible to think straight and she snatched the recipe book from his hands.

'You're not supposed to be in here!' she informed him. 'You're supposed to be out there. Working. I put a lot of effort in dragging my dressing table downstairs for you because you couldn't possibly make do with the sofa and the coffee table.'

'Now you make me sound fussy.'

Her eyes slid over to where he was picking up one of the onions, which he began to peel.

'You *are* fussy,' Jennifer grumbled. 'Most people would have made do.'

'These things are fiddly.'

'Have you never peeled an onion before?'

'Look at me and tell me what you think.'

Jennifer glanced at him. His eyes were watering and he wiped one with the back of his hand.

'You're the only woman who can make me cry like this,' he murmured. She felt warm colour flood her cheeks while she mentally slapped herself on the wrist because he was just teasing her. He'd always enjoyed teasing her. He had once told her that he liked to see her blush. Now that she had stopped sniping at him, he was once again comfortable teasing her. Still, she looked away abruptly and told him not to be silly, to leave the wretched onion alone, that too many cooks spoiled the broth...

'Ah, but many hands make light work,' he quipped, carrying on with the task, 'and it's only fair that we both share the cooking duties. Besides, it gives me an opportunity to try and persuade you to work for me. I want to lock you up and throw away the key before you have time to consider other options.'

'It's tempting,' Jennifer admitted. 'But I don't want to have anyone think that I got a job because of my connections to you. It wouldn't feel right and it would compromise my working conditions. There's such a thing as office politics, although you probably don't know that because you're the head of the pile.'

'I'd be your boss on paper but in reality you'd report through a different chain of command. The company isn't even lodged in my head office. They're housed in an old Victorian building in West London, far from the madding crowd, and I shall let them continue to lease the premises. Makes more sense than dragging them into central London. So you'd be far away from me.'

He'd moved on to the peppers and was making short work of cutting them into strips. He was quick but untidy. He was a typical male with a cavalier approach to food preparation. Bits of discarded pepper were flicked into the sink or else accidentally brushed onto the ground. He might be helping but she would spend an hour afterwards cleaning up behind him. Instead of finding the prospect of that frustrating, she had to conceal a smile of indulgence. God, what was happening to her? Were her brains in the process of being scrambled like the eggs she had cooked for him the day before?

'I don't know how much notice I would have to give my boss in Paris.' She was determined to ignore the increasingly potent effect he was having on her. 'It's usually one month but they've been very good to me and I wouldn't want to leave them in the lurch.'

'Naturally.' He looked around for something else to chop and decided to avoid the mushrooms, which looked grubby. Giving up on his good deed, he washed his hands and moved on to the less onerous task of pouring them both something to drink. A glass of wine. Rules of normality were suspended out here, so why not? He leaned against the counter and watched as she started putting things together. She didn't try and impress him with her culinary skills. Twice she apologised in advance for something she was sure would taste pretty appalling. She ignored the scales and the measuring cup. She was a breath of fresh air.

He didn't like women who went out of their way to try and impress him. He had fallen victim once, many years ago, to a woman's wiles and he had vowed never to repeat the mistake. He never had. Nothing was as off-putting as the woman who wanted to display her culinary talent. Behind that, he could always read the unspoken text. *Let me show you what a good catch I am and then maybe we could start talking about the next stage.*

For James, there was never a next stage. At least not in the foreseeable future. He supposed that one day he would start thinking about settling down, but he would recognise that day when and if it came, and so far it was nowhere on his horizon.

'And then there's the question of leaving your friends behind.' He sipped his wine and resisted the temptation to brush that wayward tendril of hair from her cheek.

'I think we'll all make the effort to keep in touch,' Jennifer said drily. She looked at her concoction and hoped for better things when it had done its time in the oven. For the moment, there was nothing else to add and she began tidying the counters, nudging him out of the way and allowing him to press the glass of wine into her hand.

James wanted to ask her how much she would miss the French fedora man but he couldn't work out how to introduce him into the conversation. Nor could he quite understand why he was bothered by the thought of her ex-boyfriend, anyway. She suddenly turned to him and he flushed to have been caught staring at her.

'So I'm assuming you're on board…'

'Yes.' She made her mind up. She wasn't going to let a once-in-a-lifetime prospect slip away from her for the wrong reasons. She wasn't going to let the past dictate the present or the future. 'I'm on board. Of course, I'll have to hear the complete package.'

'I think you'll find that it will be a generous one. Shame we have no champagne. We could have cracked a bottle open to celebrate.'

Jennifer wasn't sure of the wisdom of that. Alcohol, James and her increasingly confusing emotions didn't make good bedfellows. With the cooking out of the way, she edged to one of the kitchen chairs, sat down and watched him there by the kitchen sink, sipping his wine and contemplating her over the rim of his glass.

'And I expect you'll turn this down, but there will always be a company flat for you to stay in, should you choose.'

'You're right. I've turned it down. Ellie…my friend in London…I've maintained the rent on a room in her house. I always knew that I'd be back in London and it's there, waiting for me.' She wondered what his place was like. Did he live in a house? An apartment? She wanted the background pieces to slot together so that the picture in her head could be more complete. What did that mean?

'Do you know—' she laughed lightly '—that I don't actually know where you live in London?'

'Kensington.' And you could have known, James thought, if you had kept in touch. He pictured her in his sprawling apartment, wrestling with a cookery book and trying to turn a recipe into something appetising. He pictured her with a glass of wine in her hand, laughing that rich, full-throated laughter. The image was so sudden, so unexpected, that he shook his head to clear it and frowned.

'How lovely.' That slight frown reminded her that perhaps she was being nosy.

'Well, it's big although I'm not sure you would find it lovely.' *What would she look like sitting across from him at his dinner table? With her elbows resting on the glass surface? Laughing?*

'Why?'

'It's very modern and I know you've never liked modern things.'

'I could have changed.'

'Have you?'

'Not that much,' she admitted, swirling the drink in her glass and then taking a sip. 'That's one reason why I've continued to rent the room in Ellie's house. I love where it's located and I love the fact that it's small and cosy and Victorian. There's a garden and in summer it's absolutely beautiful.'

James thought that she would have loathed the company flat, which was modelled along the lines of his own apartment, although half the size. Pale walls, pale wooden flooring, pale furniture, abstract paintings on the walls, high-tech kitchen with all mod cons known to mankind.

'I think you should email your office and give them advance warning of your plan to return to the UK. The sooner we can get this sorted, the better.' Now that she had agreed to the job, he couldn't wait to get her to sign on the dotted line.

'And you're sure you don't want to interview anyone else for the position?'

'Never been more sure of anything in my life.'

'And how is your back feeling, James? I'm sorry I haven't asked sooner. I've just been thinking about this whole job thing...'

'A near lethal diet of painkillers is doing its job.' He walked towards her. He couldn't get images out of his mind, images of her in his apartment, images of her looking at him the way he knew he wanted to look at her, images of her turning to him, raising her lips to his, closing her eyes…

He remembered the feel of her from all those years ago when he had gently turned her away and was rocked by the realisation that he had never cleared his head of the memory. He wondered whether it was because she was so much taller and so much more voluptuously endowed than the women he had dated before and since. She had offered herself to him as a naive girl and he hadn't hesitated in turning her away because to do otherwise would have been to have taken advantage of her gullibility. Now, the offer was no longer on the cards but he wanted her. He wanted her as the woman she had become. Independent, outspoken, challenging. In every respect, so different from the airheads of his past.

When he thought about the Frenchman, he had to subdue the sudden surge of jealousy. He wasn't a jealous man and yet, there it was, the green-eyed monster buried underneath his cool.

'But the pain is still there. Might have to see the doctor when I get back to London. Might…' he leaned against the kitchen table, directly in front of her so that she had to look up to meet his eyes '…have to go to a physiotherapist. Who knows? When something happens to your back, the consequences can last for years…'

'Really?'

'Really,' he confirmed seriously. 'Which is why I'm thinking that it might be a good idea if you could maybe massage my back for me.'

'Massage your back?'

'It's a big ask but I don't want to wake up at two in the morning again in agony. I also don't want to find that when this snow's disappeared, I'm still laid up and can't get back out to work.'

'And you think a massage is going to help you?'

'I don't think it can do any harm. I wouldn't have asked you two days ago. I realise you had some kind of problem with me…'

'I didn't have a problem with you,' Jennifer said awkwardly. 'I was just surprised to find you here.'

'But we seem, thankfully, to have put whatever differences you may have had with me to rest, which is why I feel comfortable about asking you to do this…unless, of course, you'd rather not help me out here…would fully understand…'

'Well, just while the chicken's in the oven. I guess.' *Massage?* If he knew how disobedient her thoughts about him had been, that would be the last suggestion to leave his mouth. He had rejected her once. He would run a mile if he thought that there might be any temptation on her part to repeat her folly.

Not that she would. But she still felt uncertain about touching him, even in a way that wasn't sexual. What excuse would she give to shoot his request down in flames? As he had said, their differences had been overcome, they were back on safe ground, friends but without the complications of her having a crush on him… He felt nothing for her. He would wonder why she couldn't help him out, especially if, as he had intimated, the pulled muscles in his back could have lasting repercussions.

'Five minutes,' he agreed. 'It might make all the difference…'

Back in the sitting room, which was wonderfully warm with the open fire burning, James stripped off his top. In truth, his back still protested vehemently at any extreme movement, although he acknowledged that he had exaggerated just a little. He lay face down on the sofa and waited as she pulled a couple of cushions over so that she could kneel on the ground next to him.

His skin was cool as she began kneading his firm, bronzed back. He had the perfect physique. Broad shoulders, tapering to a narrow waist and long, muscular legs. There was a mantra playing in her head, one she was forcing herself to repeat: *He's just a friend, how nice to be pals once again, pals always help each other out...*

She could feel his body relax under the pressure of her fingers. She, on the other hand, couldn't be further from relaxed. Her pulses were in free fall and her heart was racing so fast that she could scarcely breathe properly. It was just as well his back was to her. If not, she was certain that he would be able to see the telltale traces of a woman...

Turned on. She stopped massaging and informed him that she would have to check the chicken.

'Surely it won't be ready yet.' He turned over before she had time to stand up and suddenly she was no longer safely staring at his back but instead looking straight at him, lying there, sexily semi clad. 'Raw chicken...not recommended by any major chef...'

'Yes...well...' There was no way that she would allow her eyes to drift down to his bare chest and even meeting his eyes with some semblance of self-control was a trial.

'That felt good.'

Jennifer licked her lips nervously. There was a subtle change in the atmosphere. He was holding her glance for too long and she couldn't tear her eyes away from his. The mantra had fragmented into worthless pieces and she was only aware of the changes in her body as he continued to stare at her.

'Sit.' He shifted his big body a little and patted a space next to him on the sofa. Idiotically, Jennifer obeyed. She wasn't quite sure why.

Her fingers were resting lightly on her lap and she nearly passed out when he reached to entwine his fingers with hers, although he didn't take his eyes away from her face.

Jennifer found that she was nailed to the sofa as he began doing that thing with his thumb, rubbing it gently on her hand so that her breathing became jerky and uneven and her mouth went dry.

When the silence became too much to bear, she finally found her voice and said, shakily, 'What are you doing?' She didn't want to look at their enmeshed fingers because to do that would have been to acknowledge that she knew exactly what he was doing. Caressing her. Was it some kind of weird *thank-you-great-massage* caress? Was he aware of what it was doing to her? Was this a *friendly thing*?

'I'm touching you,' James murmured in a voice that implied that he was as surprised by the gesture as she was. 'Do you want me to stop?'

Jennifer was having trouble getting past the first part of his statement. This was what she had seemingly spent a lifetime fantasising about. The four years she had spent telling herself that daydreams played no part in reality, that he had never been attracted to her, that she had to *wake up and smell the coffee*, floated away like early morning mist on a summer day.

'Yes! No…this isn't…isn't appropriate…'

'Why isn't it?'

'You know why...' There was a very good reason but she couldn't quite remember what exactly it was and, while she was trying to figure it out, he drew her slowly down towards him.

A buzz of nervous excitement ripped through her. She was the kid opening her eyes on Christmas Day, wondering if the much-longed-for present would live up to expectation... She knew that no good would come of any physical contact with him, that she wanted, had always wanted so much more than he could ever offer, and yet his pull was magnetic and irresistible and her curiosity and raw longing far too powerful.

She closed her eyes on a soft sigh and their mouths touched, a sweetly exploring caress, then he reached both his hands into her hair, brushed his thumbs along her neck and didn't give her the opportunity to surface as the gentle exploration turned into something wonderfully, erotically hungry.

Jennifer lowered herself onto him and her breasts squashed against his chest. In between drowning in his kisses, she surfaced to tell him in a shaky voice that they really shouldn't be doing this...that he wasn't himself... that the chicken in the oven was going to burn...

He, for his part, laughed softly and informed her that this was exactly what they should be doing.

His hand had moved from the nape of her neck to slide underneath her top. He stroked her back, his hand moving upwards until he was brushing her bra strap. He carried on kissing her while he unclasped it.

'I'm not one of your Polly Pockets...' Along with a shudder of intense excitement, she felt the hangover of self-consciousness that had always afflicted her in his presence. He liked them little. She wasn't.

'Stop talking,' James commanded huskily. 'Let me see you.'

Jennifer arched up into an awkward sitting position and he shoved her top up. Bountiful breasts tumbled out, breasts that were much more than a handful, breasts a man could lose himself in. He groaned.

'I've died and gone to heaven,' he breathed unevenly. Her nipples peeped over the unclasped bra. With her head flung back and her long, curly hair tumbling down her back, she was the epitome of sexiness, a wanton goddess the likes of which he had never seen before.

Once she had offered herself to him. Only now could he receive that offering. He touched the tips of her nipples with his fingers, circling them and trying not to explode with desire as the tips firmed and stiffened in response. She was panting and moaning softly, little noises that inflamed him. He didn't know how long he would be able to indulge in foreplay because he was losing his self-control fast. When she edged upwards on the sofa so that her breasts now dangled provocatively close to his mouth, he circled her waist with his hands, determined to take things as slowly as he could.

It felt like an impossible task, requiring heroic efforts beyond his control, as he gently levered her down so that he could suckle on a proffered nipple. He drew the pulsing bud into his mouth and luxuriated in tasting her. He was a big man with big hands and her lush breasts suited them perfectly. How could he ever have been satisfied with those thin women with jutting hip bones and small breasts?

The sofa was big but they still had to wriggle to find comfortable positions. While they did, he continued sucking her nipples and massaging her breasts. He could have carried on for ever.

'This sofa isn't ideal,' he broke free to tell her.

'I can lay the duvet in front of the fire…'

'Do it without your clothes on. I want to see every naked inch of your perfect body.'

Jennifer stood up and slowly stripped off her clothes. She wasn't inexperienced but removing every item of clothing while her man looked on with rampantly appreciative eyes was new to her. She felt deliciously, thrillingly wanton. He had been vocal in his praise for her body, had lavished attention on breasts that were big by anyone's standards, had hoarsely told her that she was beautiful. Any lingering self-consciousness she might have had had disappeared under the onslaught of his compliments. In fact, she felt heady and sexy and bursting with self-confidence.

As she began pushing aside the coffee table that sat in the centre of the room, making space for the king-sized, thick, soft duvet, he told her to take her time. When it was time for her to fetch the duvet from the sofa, he stood up and began undressing, more slowly than he might have had his back not still been aching.

The breath caught in her throat as the images she had stored in her head were replaced by the reality. When he was completely naked, he held her eyes and then motioned for her to look at him as he touched himself. He was a big man and everything about him was impressively big, including the erection his hand circled.

In her wildest, fiercest day dreams, she had never imagined that it could feel so good to be standing here, naked, on the brink of making love to this man. She walked over to him and removed his hand so that she could replace it with her own. To feel him throb against the palm of her hand…

Was she doing the right thing? Never had anything felt

so right. She stretched up to kiss him and this time they kissed long and tenderly.

'You'll have to do the work,' he murmured, breaking free and leading her towards the duvet. 'Don't forget that I'm a man with a bad back...'

'I wouldn't want to do further damage,' Jennifer returned, guiding his hand to her breast. 'I remember what you said about bad backs never going away...'

'I'd be happy to swap the health of my back for an hour in bed with you.'

How easy it would be to allow words she'd never thought she would ever hear to get to her. How easy to lose herself in the excitement of the moment. A little core of practical common sense cautioned her against jumping into this wonderful situation feet first, without any thought for rocks that might lie beneath.

This was what she wanted. She had waited a long time and she knew now that she had spent the past four years waiting. How long would she have waited? She didn't know. But that didn't mean that this was the beginning of every dream she had ever had coming true. That wasn't how life worked.

They lay down on the duvet, which was mercifully soft.

She curved her body against his, drawing her leg over his thigh, and riffled his dark hair with her fingers.

When she looked at his impossibly handsome face, she saw the past entwined with the present, the boy as he had been and the man he had become. The feelings she had had for him, which had started with the sweet innocence of infatuation, had grown and matured and had never gone away. Being thrown together in the cottage had made her realise that. What she felt for him was no longer infatuation. Neither had it been four years ago. Infatuation didn't have much of a life span; it would have faded over time, replaced by other experiences.

She loved him and she knew, without quite understanding why, that any mention of love would have him running for cover. She took this on board and knew that she still wanted to be right here with him, even if her feelings left her exposed and vulnerable.

'You are beautiful,' he interrupted her chain of thoughts and she smiled sadly.

'I don't want to kill the moment, but that's not what you said four years ago.'

'Four years ago you were a child.'

'I was twenty-one!'

'A very young twenty-one,' James murmured, stroking her hair away from her face. 'Too young for someone as jaded as me. You've grown up in the past four years, Jennifer.'

Grown up but still as vulnerable as that twenty-one-year-old girl had been. She nodded and kissed him and pushed uncomfortable thoughts to the back of her mind. Her nipple tingled and throbbed as it rubbed against his chest. She straddled him and eased her body up so that when she lowered it he could take her nipple into his mouth and suckle on it until her body was alive with sensation. She groaned as he slipped his hand between her legs and began caressing her, rubbing fingers along the sensitised, slippery groove until she could hardly bear the exquisite, agonising need to be completely fulfilled.

'Not fair,' she murmured into his mouth, but she moved her hips sensuously against his exploring hand and he laughed with rich appreciation.

'I want to taste you,' he groaned, easing her into an upright position so that she was kneeling over him and he could fully take in the beauty of her spectacular body.

Her heavy breasts were amazing, her nipples dark and perfectly formed and the patch of dark hair nestled between her thighs was as sweet and aromatic as honey. He clasped her from behind and nudged her closer to his mouth.

Jennifer rested her hands flat against his shoulders and shuddered at the first touch of his tongue tasting her. He took his time, licking and exploring and then falling back when she thought she couldn't take any more. She was cresting a wave except, just when the wave threatened to break, it simply ebbed and began building again. It was the most incredible experience. She had wondered what it would be like to be with him. Nothing like this. This was way, way better than anything she had conjured up in her head.

'I can't take any more of this,' she gasped, when he had, once again, brought her almost to the point of no return.

She slid off him to lie on her side where she could try and let her breathing return to normal, but how could it when he was nudging his thigh between hers and sending her right back to the brink?

'I can't take much more myself,' James admitted shakily. 'I never lose control but I'm in danger of doing so very soon.'

'Shall I see how much stamina you have…?'

She wriggled around so that while he explored her with his mouth, she could likewise explore him with hers. He was rock hard and tasting him made her want to swoon, as did his continuing exploration of the delicate groove between her legs.

Their mutual need was frantic by the time her mouth joined his in a wet, musky, greedy kiss.

'I need you. Now.'

And I love you so much, was the reply that flew through her head. 'I need you too,' she returned huskily.

'Are you protected?'

'I'm not at the moment but I can be…'

CHAPTER SIX

JENNIFER'S bag was lying on the ground next to the chair. She unzipped it and rustled in the side pocket where a memento of that non-event four years ago lay. The condom, optimistically bought and never used for a love-making session that had never happened, had been through a lot. It had jostled next to coins and make-up and packets of chewing gum. It had been transferred from bag to bag, a secret talisman and a permanent reminder of her youthful foolishness. It had even drowned and been resuscitated when, on a boat trip with her father in Majorca, she had accidentally dropped her bag in the sea.

Fetching it out of its compartment felt like fate.

'Not yet.' He caught her hand as she was about to tear open the little packet. 'My back feels up to a little bit more foreplay…'

In truth, he felt fighting fit and this time she was the one lying on the duvet as he explored every glorious inch of her succulent body. She tossed beneath him and he pinned her down, subjecting her to the onslaught of his mouth and tongue and hands. Their bodies were slick with perspiration when, unable to take any more, she cried out for him to enter her.

The condom that had been through the wars was finally serving its purpose and as he thrust into her she bucked and cried out in ecstasy. The feel of him inside her was beyond all expectations. He was big and powerful and he filled her in a way she would never have dreamed possible. It was as if their bodies were made for each other. They moved in perfect rhythm and her orgasm, when she finally came, was wave upon wave of such pleasure that her whole body quivered and shook from the strength of it.

The used condom joined the logs burning in the open fire and she curved her body against his with a gurgle of contentment.

'Amazing,' James murmured softly. 'It's done my back a world of good. I think we'll have to carry on with this method of physiotherapy if I'm to improve and suffer no lasting damage.'

Jennifer had never felt so blissfully happy and completely whole. For the first time in her life, her body was complete.

Then she wondered how long the physiotherapy was destined to continue. She glanced outside through the window and the snow reminded her that this was a snatched moment in time.

'Pretty incredible.' She brushed his cheek with her hand. He had shaved earlier but she could feel the stubble already trying to make a reappearance. She nuzzled his chin and settled on top of him so that she could feel every inch of his body underneath her.

'Everything you dreamed of?' There was laughter in his voice but the navy-blue eyes were solemn.

'I'm not going to feed your ego by telling you how great it was, James.' She unglued herself from him to allow his hands to wedge over her breasts where he could tease her nipples.

'Cruel woman.' He laughed out loud this time and continued to roll the pads of his thumbs over her nipples, which were already standing to attention even though it had only been minutes since they had been lavished with devotion. 'I'm tempted to punish you by not allowing you to get any sleep tonight. In fact, if I had my way I wouldn't let you leave my side…'

And he almost succeeded in doing just that. At least for the next forty-eight hours, during which the snow began to slacken in its fury and the unremitting leaden grey skies gradually showed glimpses of pale, milky blue.

Jennifer yielded to the bubble in which there were just the two of them, playing house like babes in the wood and making love wherever and whenever, which was everywhere and often. Her one condom had done its job but James had more at the house because he would never, she assumed, take risks of any kind with any woman.

He told her repeatedly that he couldn't get enough of her and, with every smile and every touch, she fell deeper and deeper into love. It consumed her and it was only when, lying on her bed, wrapped up with him, she looked outside and noticed that the snow had finally and completely stopped.

'It's not snowing any longer,' she said and James followed her gaze to see that she was right. He hadn't even noticed. In fact, over the past three days there was a great deal that he hadn't noticed. Starting with the state of the weather and ending with his work, which he had rudimentarily covered. Most of the time, his computer lay on the dressing table, which neither of them had bothered to relocate to the bedroom, untouched.

'If I know anything about the weather here, we'll wake up tomorrow morning to find bright sunshine and the snow melted.'

She couldn't prevent a certain wistfulness from creeping into her voice because with the end of the snow came the beginning of the questions that she had conveniently put to one side. What happened next? Where did they go from here? Was this a relationship or was it only a consequence of the fact that they had been cooped up for days on end?

She wasn't about to start asking questions, though.

James was adept at picking up the intonations in women's voices. He waited for her to continue and frowned when there was nothing forthcoming.

'I don't want you to return to Paris,' he surprised himself by saying, and Jennifer looked at him in astonishment.

'Well, we can't stay here for ever pretending the rest of the world doesn't exist,' she pointed out. She turned back to face the window, resting in the crook of his arm. The moon was big and fat and round and it filled the bedroom with a silvery glow.

James was accustomed to women making demands on his time. It irritated him that she made no attempt to demand anything. Having spent the past few days living purely for the moment, he was now driven to get inside her head and discover what she was thinking. He had just nailed his colours to the mast and told her that he wanted her to quit her job immediately for him, and was her only response to be that they couldn't stay put and block out the rest of the world? As if that were the only logical option to ditching her Paris placement?

'I'm not implying that we should do that,' he said edgily. 'But we're going to have to start thinking about leaving here…and we're going to have to decide what happens with us now.'

'Maybe we should go our separate ways,' Jennifer told him. He might want her to give up her job immediately but that was just him reaching out and taking what he wanted without a scrap of thought for what *she* wanted. She had been a keen observer of his girlfriends down the years. None of them had ever lasted longer than a holiday. He had taken what he wanted from them and discarded them when he thought that it was time to move on.

'You mean that?' He raised himself up and spun her round to look at him because he wanted her undivided attention.

'Look, you're not into long-term relationships—'

'And that's what you want?'

Of course it was! But she knew what would happen next if she were to say that. His pursuit, such as it was, would come to a grinding halt. She might play hard to get, but, really and truly, did she want this to end so abruptly? Eventually, it would, but why shouldn't she enjoy herself for as long as she could and let tomorrow take care of it-self? She hated the weakness behind that choice but even more she hated the hypocrisy of pretending that it would be worthwhile to walk away now and become a martyr to her principles.

'Let me finish,' she inserted, picking and choosing her words very carefully. 'We…this…I guess, for me, this is unfinished business…'

'Unfinished business?' He flung aside the duvet and strode towards the window to glare outside at the picture-postcard winter scene before swinging around to scowl at her. 'I'm *unfinished business*?'

'Okay, maybe I didn't phrase that quite as well as I should have…'

She sat up and drew her legs up. 'Come back to bed. I…I…' Some truth forced its way out. 'I don't want to go back to Paris either,' she confessed, at which he slowly returned to lie down next to her.

'Then pack it in. Tell them something. Anything. I want you here with me.'

'Yes…it's fun…it would be nice to carry on seeing one another, I guess…' *But for how long?* That was a question that was definitely off the cards. 'I mean, no strings attached, of course…'

He could feel a return of that groundswell of dissatisfaction, the same dissatisfaction that had slammed into him when she had labelled him as *unfinished business*, and he couldn't understand why because what she was saying tuned in perfectly with his own personal philosophy. No strings attached had been his motto for a very long time. And wasn't she, in her own way, his unfinished business as well? Something had been started four years ago and it had now reached fruition.

'I never took you for a *no-strings-attached* kind of girl.'

Jennifer stilled. He knew her so well, but did she want him to ever suspect how much he meant to her? Did she really want to open herself up to being hurt all over again? She couldn't face his pity for a second time.

'It just shows how much you have to learn about me,' she murmured lightly.

'So you'll email your Paris office…bid them a fond adieu…?'

'I'll go and discuss the matter with my boss over there,' she said firmly.

'I don't know how long I can wait before you return. If we're talking in terms of months, then forget it. I'll go over there myself and drag you back to London.'

He propped himself up on one elbow, rested his hand on her stomach and traced the outline of her belly button. Jennifer, caught in the now familiar tide of longing, fought to stay in control.

'Do you always get your own way when it comes to women?' she asked breathlessly, staring straight up at the ceiling and not pushing him away when he dipped his fingers lower to sift the soft, downy hair between her thighs. Before he could start doing even more dramatic things to her body, things that always seemed to wreak havoc with her thought processes, she wriggled onto her side so that their bodies mirrored one another, both of them propped up on their elbows, staring directly into each other's eyes. She didn't want to get hopelessly lost in making love. She wanted to talk, really talk.

'I can't tell a lie...'

'What do they hope for?' she asked in genuine bewilderment. She knew what *she* hoped for, but she was a lost cause and had been from as far back as she could remember. Other women, women he had gone out with for a matter of a few weeks, surely they couldn't all be silly enough to think they could tie him down? Or was he only attracted to women like himself, women who wanted affairs and were happy to part company when the lust bit was exhausted?

'What do you mean?'

'Do they honestly think that you're going to offer them a lasting relationship?'

'How can they?' James said impatiently. 'The women I date always know from the beginning that I'm not interested in walking down the aisle. Why are we having this discussion, anyway? When we both agree that you're going to leave Paris immediately and come back here...'

Jennifer ignored his interruption. 'And they don't mind?'

'I suppose,' James admitted grudgingly, 'there are instances when one of them might have wanted to take things to another level, but, as far as I am concerned, if a woman chooses to go out with me, then she chooses what she's signing up for.' *No-strings-attached fun...* He swept aside the unsettling memory of how her easy acceptance of that had thrown him.

'And you've never been tempted?'

'You talk too much,' he growled.

'You'll have to get used to it.'

'You never used to ask so many questions.'

'I never used to ask *any* questions…but then again, we were never in the place we are now, were we?'

'I've never been tempted.' He lay back and shielded his face with his arm, then he pulled her against him and slung his arm around her shoulder so that the tips of his fingers were brushing her nipple, although his mind appeared to be far away.

'You probably don't remember when my father died,' he surprised her by saying. 'You would have been…what… fifteen? It was a pretty terrible time all round. Daisy was in pieces.'

'I remember. You abandoned your gap year and went to work. It was tough. I know.'

'They had just lost their figurehead. The employees were edgy and so was the bank. I'd worked there before, summer jobs…well, you know that.' He felt her nod against him and he inhaled deeply. He had always thought it a myth that confessions were good for the soul, so why was he telling her this? 'I knew a bit about the accounts but I was green around the ears. Like it or not, though, I was a majority shareholder and responsibility fell on my shoulders.'

'And you were still grieving for your dad… How hard that must have been, James…' Her heart went out to him because, however mature he might have been for his age, he had still only been a kid, really, one forced to grow up very, very quickly.

'It was...very hard. I was in a bad place. I got involved with a woman.'

'You *got involved with a woman*?'

'You say that as though I started growing two heads and five arms,' James said drily. This was new ground for him. This window in his life had always been kept a secret. No one, including his mother, knew about that indiscretion ten or so years ago. He had never been tempted to confide in any of the women he had dated, even though they had all pressed him for details of his personal life as though getting beneath the armour would guarantee a foot through the door.

Jennifer had a moment of feeling special until he continued in the same flat, neutral voice, 'And the reason I'm telling you now, aside from the fact that we go back a long way, is that I want you to understand why I've made the choices that I've made with women.'

Jennifer was still trying to work out which woman he was talking about. She remembered that time quite clearly, although it was many years ago. He had lost the easy banter and the light-hearted teasing and was beginning the transition to the man he would later become. Controlled, single-minded, adept at channelling his incredible intelligence towards a single goal and getting there whatever it took. For the first time he had been around and yet she had hardly seen him.

'I thought you were completely wrapped up with the company,' she said, looking at him. 'When would you have had time to go out socialising? Dad and I nicknamed you The Invisible Man because we knew you were around but we just never saw you.'

'Well, I didn't go out socializing. The socialising came to find *me*.'

'What are you talking about?'

'Anita Hayward was the accounts manager. She looked like something that had just stepped off the cover of a magazine. Long legs, long hair, long lingering looks whenever she came into my father's office where I had set up camp. She struck just the right note between sympathy and a matter-of-fact acceptance that, tragic though the circumstances were, life had to go on. It was a break from seeing the pity in everyone's eyes and hearing the sympathy oozing in their voices. It seemed to be what I needed at that moment in time. She made it her mission to fill me in on everything that was going on in the office. I was sharp enough to know the mechanics of how things worked but I knew nothing about the people and I needed to get them onside. Twenty-minute briefings at the end of the day turned into dinners out.'

'Your mum said that you were working at the company, making sure that loose ends were tied up…but you weren't working…'

'Nope. I was being worked over.'

'What do you mean?'

James had intended to throw her the bare bones. It was more than he had ever thrown anyone else. Now, as he lay flat on his back and stared up at the ceiling, he was reliving a time he had relegated to history.

'I should have been at home. At least, I should have been at home more than I was. Instead, I was being seduced by Anita Hayward of the long red hair and the slanting green eyes.'

'And you still feel guilty…' Jennifer deduced slowly.

'Very good, Sherlock.'

'But no one operates on all cylinders when they're experiencing great stress. We react in different ways. What… what happened…in the end?'

'In the end,' he said drily, 'I discovered that she was

after a promotion. It was as simple as that. I had been used by an ambitious woman who wanted to make sure that she got the top job when the cabinet was reshuffled. And by the way, she had a boyfriend. I caught them in one of the directors' offices when I happened to return to the building after hours because I'd forgotten something. Either the boyfriend was in on the game or else he was just another sap she was using for her own ends. The fact is that, at a crucial time in my life, I took my eye off the ball.'

He turned to her, cupped her breast in his hand and Jennifer covered his hand with hers.

'You use sex as a substitute for talking,' she told him and he smiled crookedly at her.

'And you talk too much.'

'So…because of one unfortunate experience, you decided…what…?'

'I like the way you describe that wrong turn as an unfortunate experience… Well, because of that unfortunate experience, I made a rational decision to steer clear of anything called uncontrolled emotional involvement.'

For Jennifer, the long line of airhead blondes now made a lot of sense. He had fallen in love, or *thought* he had fallen in love, with a woman who was sensitive, intelligent, beautiful and mature, and, for his trouble, he had ended up being manipulated at a time when he had been at his most vulnerable. He had emerged from the experience with the building blocks for a fortress and behind the walls of that fortress he had sealed away any part of him that could be touched. The women he had dated since had been disposable and she would be as well.

Realistically, she might last a bit longer because of their history, because they had slightly more going for them than just sex, but she, like the rest of them, would be disposable.

'What happened to her?' Jennifer asked, and when he replied she could hear the ice in his voice.

'She got the sack. Not immediately, of course, and not directly. There are all sorts of regulations pertaining to employee dismissal. No, she was treated to a series of sideways moves. The vertical line she had manoeuvred towards suddenly flattened out and became horizontal. Removing myself from the equation, she failed to realise that there was no way I could have someone working for me who was capable of deceit. Strangely enough, even after I caught them having sex on the desk, she continued to believe that she could patch things over and pick up where we had left off. When she realised that her career in my company was over, she decided to lay all her cards on the table. Not only had she slept with me to further her career but she was no young girl of twenty-four with a ladder to climb and a sackful of qualifications. She was thirty-three and I later found out that most of her qualifications had been fabricated.'

'I'm sorry,' Jennifer said quietly and he shrugged against her.

'Why? We all need a learning curve in our lives.'

Jennifer, resting against him, thought that she had already had hers except she seemed to have learnt nothing from it. He had once rejected her and she had thought she had learnt to keep away and yet here she was, in his arms and busy repeating the same process, except this time the hole she had dug for herself was a lot deeper.

'And you've told me this because...you want to warn me off getting too involved with you,' she surmised thoughtfully. 'You don't have to worry on that score.'

'Because I'm your unfinished business?'

'I'm sorry that you found that offensive. I'd always wondered...'

'You don't have to explain, Jen. I've wondered too.'

'You have?'

'I'm only human. Of course I have. I had very graphic dreams about you for a long time after that incident.'

'What was I doing in those dreams?'

'When you're back in London and we have the benefit of a bed with a wrought-iron bedstead and some cloth, I'll demonstrate...'

As she had predicted from past experience, the snow stopped abruptly overnight and the temperatures rose sufficiently for the settled snow to start thawing.

They went to sleep that night and by the following evening, the outlines and contours of the fields around the house and cottage were slipping back into focus. His back was still not in top condition but between them they could clear the drive and he disappeared up to the house to get his car, which he drove down to the cottage. There was snow on the roof and the bonnet but it was melting almost as she looked at it.

In the space of a few days, she felt as though her well-ordered life had been turned on its head. She had grown, developed, matured and become an ambitious, successful and single-minded career woman in Paris, but emotionally she now thought that she had been sleepwalking. She hadn't moved on from James, she had just held herself in abeyance until they met again.

He wanted her to quit her job but he had been careful to give her no promises of a future. They would be lovers. He had treated her the same way he had treated all the women he had ever gone out with. Up front announcing his lack of commitment, making sure she didn't get it into her head that long term was part of his vocabulary.

By the time they left the estate, the insurance company had been contacted and she had also spoken to her father and emailed him a list of things that would need doing when he returned.

As James drove them away she looked back at the disappearing cottage as though it had been a dream. When she turned to look ahead, she wondered how she was going to fare in the real world and, as though sensing her doubts, James rested his hand over hers and flicked her a sideways glance.

'I've been thinking. Perhaps I should come with you to Paris. It's been a while since I had a holiday...'

Jennifer had had time to think about everything. From her perspective, she had run into her past and discovered that she had never managed to escape it after all. Locked away in the cottage, she had found how fast a youthful crush could turn into hopeless adult love. She had had no weapons at her disposal powerful enough to protect her against the man who had stolen her heart a thousand years ago.

She wasn't, however, stupid. James liked her. He certainly adored her body. That was where the story ended. He had warned her off looking for anything more than sex and she had successfully convinced him that they were both on the same wavelength.

She didn't have enough good sense to walk away from him but she had enough good sense to know that when the time came for them to go their separate ways, she wanted to be able to do so with her head held high.

'Come with me to Paris?' she said now. 'James...Paris isn't going to be *a holiday*.'

James stifled a surge of irritation. 'I realise you're going to be working but it wouldn't be beyond the realms of possibility for me to arrange to be in Paris for a week or so.'

Bliss, Jennifer thought. That would be absolute bliss. Getting back to her little apartment, knowing that she would be seeing him later. Cooking together and showing him all the little cafés and restaurants where the owners knew her, taking him to that special *boulangerie* that sold the best bread in the city and the markets where they could stock up on fresh fruit and vegetables and tease each other about who could concoct the most edible meal. She could introduce him to her friends and afterwards they could lie in bed and make love and he could tell her what he thought of them in that witty, sharp, amusing way of his... *Bliss*.

The pleasant daydream fell away in pieces. She knew, without a shadow of a doubt, that if she was to take that first step down the road of doing whatever he wanted it would the first step down a very slippery slope.

'You've been out of your office for several days. How on earth would you be able to wangle a week-long trip to Paris?'

A slashing smile of satisfaction curved his lips. 'Because I'm the boss. I call the shots. It's an undeniable perk of the job. Besides, I've always maintained the importance of having good people to whom responsibility can be delegated. I have a queue of people lining up to prove to me how capable they are of covering in my absence.'

'Well, I'm sorry but I don't think it would be a very good idea.'

'Why not?' He slipped his hand between her legs and pushed his knuckles against her and the pressure was so arousing that she began to dampen in her underwear. The past few days had taught her that he was an intensely physical man. He relied on his ability to arouse to make his point and to win his arguments and it would have been so easy to let him have his way.

He returned his hand to the steering wheel. He couldn't keep his hands off her and he knew that she felt the same

way about him. There were times when he looked at her
and he knew, from the faint blush on her cheeks, that if he
reached out and felt her she would be hot and wet for him.
So what, he wondered with baffled exasperation, was the
problem in capitalising on the time they spent together?

'I feel badly enough about leaving everyone there in
the lurch.'

'You're not leaving them *in the lurch*,' James pointed
out irritably. 'They understood perfectly the circumstances
surrounding your resignation. Your father's getting older...
the emergency at the cottage further proof that you will
be needed here more and more over time... The fact that
there's the offer of a job that might not be on the cards
for ever and you owe it to yourself and your father that
you take it while it's there... You've offered to see in your
successor and train them up. Why would you think that
they're being left in the lurch?'

'Because I do.'

'That's insane feminine logic.'

Jennifer clicked her tongue and sighed because he could
be so *black and white*.

'From my perspective,' he continued, proving to her
how well she knew his thought processes, 'you've acted
in the most sensible, practical way possible.'

'Well, I don't want you around distracting me.'

'But you know how much fun a bit of distraction can
be...' James murmured, savouring that small admission
of weakness from her. They were few and far between.
Much to his annoyance.

'I'll be there for two weeks. Maybe three. Not long.
Enough time to clear my desk, pack up the things in
my apartment I've gathered over the years, go out with
friends...'

Which, to his further annoyance, was something else

on his mind. The goodbyes to the old friends…everyone knew about *making love one last time for old times' sake*… He swept aside that ridiculous concern. Hell, she wasn't like that! But he was scowling at the mere hint of any such thing, the mere suggestion in his head that she might be tempted to go to bed with the good friend and ex-lover artist of the fedora and the earring.

Jennifer saw that scowl and smiled because, even though she knew where he stood on matters of the heart, his unrestrained possessiveness still gave her a little quiver of satisfaction. She hugged it to herself and savoured it for a few seconds.

'So let me get this straight,' he gritted. 'You don't want me in Paris and you also don't want either of us to tell our parents about what's going on…' It wasn't cool to behave like a petulant teenager and he forced a tight smile, which he was pretty sure wasn't fooling anyone.

'Well, I explained why I thought it wasn't such a good idea to tell Dad and Daisy,' Jennifer said vaguely. Her father knew her better than anyone else. He would never buy the fiction that she was the sort of girl who would indulge in something passing and insignificant with the guy who had stolen her vulnerable teenage heart. He would immediately know that she was in too deep. There would be questions and speculation and she wouldn't be able to wriggle out of telling him the truth.

'And I explained why I didn't get it.'

'I'm practical.' She began listing the reasons once again while her treacherous mind broke its leash and started imagining how wonderful it would be if she could shout her love out to the whole world. 'We both are…we know that this is just about having fun, so why drag other people into it?' She and James, lovers and in love, building a future together…she and Daisy planning a wedding, nothing too big…just the local church…friends and neighbours… 'It would just make it awkward when the inevitable happened.'

'Nice to know you're planning the demise of what we have before we've even begun.'

'These are *your* rules, James. You don't do involvement.' He couldn't argue with that. She was the perfect woman for him. She challenged him intellectually, which he found he enjoyed, and they were brilliant in bed together. In fact, they couldn't have been more compatible. She also respected his boundaries. There had been no coy insinuations about the importance of commitment, no leading questions that involved long-term planning, no shadow of disappointment when he had told her about his ill-timed disastrous affair with Anita and the consequences of it. Nor had she tried to lecture him on the importance of letting go of the past. In that respect, she ticked all the boxes.

He wondered why he wasn't feeling more pleasantly satisfied.

'Besides—' she thought it a good idea to move on from the commitment angle, just in case he got scared that she was hinting that *she did do commitment* and *preferably with him* '—we've both agreed that we're not each other's type…' Or something like that. The night before, when the conversation had mysteriously returned to Patric, even though he was no longer in her life *in that way.* James seemed obsessed with Patric and she couldn't understand why unless it was to confirm his singular position in her life, with no spectres at the feast. He wanted her in place and at his beck and call, without distractions from anyone, even an ex-lover, although, in return, she knew that he would never give those assurances back to her. The playing field would never be level as far as James went.

'So I'm not trying to sabotage what we have,' she concluded. 'We both know that this is just physical attraction.
It'll pass in time and we'll both move on so why involve
other people when there's no need?'

'Why indeed?' James grated.

'Let's just have fun. And no complications…'

CHAPTER SEVEN

JAMES glanced at his watch for the third time in ten minutes. She was running late, which was unusual for her, but he didn't mind. For the first time in nearly three and a half months, she had actually suggested meeting up, as opposed to waiting for him to take the lead. She had called him on his mobile and he had immediately booked dinner at an exclusive restaurant where, and this was just one of the upsides of wealth and power, his request for a secluded table at the back was instantly accommodated.

Of course, despite the fact that he had always loathed a woman who tried to insinuate him into a social life he didn't want and engineer arrangements without plenty of prior notice, it annoyed him that Jennifer was so completely the opposite.

She engineered nothing. She was impossible to impress. She declined his gifts. She was irritatingly elusive. Twice she had laughingly turned down his invitations to the theatre because *she was busy* and then failed to come up with an explanation why. Busy doing what? Once she had bailed on him claiming tiredness. Admittedly, he had telephoned her at short notice, in fact at eleven o'clock at night, but after a series of exhaustive meetings the only person he had wanted to see had been her. In fact, he had brought the meetings to a summary conclusion because visions of her lying naked in bed had been too much. He had failed to laugh along when she had told him, yawning, that he couldn't possibly come over because a girl needed her beauty sleep.

She wasn't playing hard to get. Far from it. When they were together, she was everything a man could wish for. She made him laugh, turned him on to the point where he was capable of forgetting everything, argued like a vixen if she didn't agree with something he said and had no qualms in teasing him on the grounds that everyone needed to be taken down a peg or two now and again. She didn't play games. She was up front in everything she did and everything she said. He had had no option but to swallow down his intense irritation when she failed to put him first.

And she never talked about a future. Everything was done on a spur-of-the-moment basis and he had gradually, inexorably and frustratingly come to the conclusion that, however sexy and accommodating she could be, he was a stopgap. When he thought about that for too long, he could feel a slow anger begin to build so he didn't think about it. Instead, he told himself that that was a good thing because stopgaps didn't lead to attachments and attachments, as he had made perfectly clear to her at the beginning of their relationship, were not on the horizon. Clearly they weren't on hers either.

A waiter came to refill his drink, a full-bodied red wine, asked him if there was anything, *anything at all*, they could bring for him while he waited for his companion. The chef, they assured him, would be more than happy to concoct some special delicacies, nothing heavy, perhaps something creative with the excellent fois gras they had only today taken delivery of...

James waved the man aside and turned on his iPad.

He sipped his red wine while lazily scrolling through

the pictures in front of him. Pictures of a house, neatly positioned in one of the leafy London suburbs, within handy commuting distance of the offices. Not a flashy apartment, which Jennifer accused his place of being... no porter sitting at the front behind a marble desk, which she found impersonal...no opulent artificial plants in the foyer, which she exclaimed weren't nearly as good as the real thing and must take for ever to dust, what a waste of someone's time.

A house in the suburbs that was already part of his vast property portfolio, which had last been rented out over a year ago and which had dropped off the radar since then. It couldn't compete with the ultra-modern places more centrally located, which appealed to expensive overseas executives. It had been brought to his attention by one of his people three weeks previously as just one of a batch to be considered for sale. He had pulled it out, seen it personally himself and made his decision on the spot to hang onto it. With some decent refurbishment, it would be perfect, and he had relished the thought of how delighted she would be at being able to move out of her poky shared house to a charming little cottage with a small but well-developed garden, a butcher, a baker and a candlestick maker within walking distance and a busy but distinct village atmosphere. Since then he had sent an expensive team of decorators in and it had been transformed, updated, modernised but retained its period style, which was the only stipulation he had made to the head of the design team. Perfect.

To think that six months earlier he might have sold it! Who said that life wasn't full of happy coincidences?

He sat back and contemplated, with satisfaction, the excitement on her face that he predicted he would see when he told her the good news. Whatever rent she was paying, he would make sure to charge less. In fact, he would happily charge nothing but he doubted she would accept that, given her stubbornness and her pride. It would be a done deal and he would no longer have to make allowances for her friend every time he visited her, tiptoeing just in case Ellie was asleep, making sure not to drink wine that wasn't Jennifer's or open beer that belonged to Ellie's boyfriend. Job done.

He glanced up, saw her hesitating by the door of the restaurant, casting her eyes around for him, and he turned off the computer, leaving it on the table next to him.

God, she was sex on legs. He had told her to don her finery, that the restaurant was one of the top ones in London, and she had. Winter was finally beginning to lose its icy winter edge as spring made itself felt and she was wearing a slim-fitting, figure-hugging dress in deep reds and browns with a pashmina artfully arranged loosely over her shoulders. Her curves seemed to grow more luscious by the day and his body was predictably reacting to the sway of her walk as she spotted him, to the sight of her cleavage, which even the modest neckline of the dress couldn't quite hide because her breasts were so lush and abundant.

For the first time, Jennifer watched James's lazy assessing smile and, instead of feeling thrilled, she felt the knot of tension in her stomach tighten.

How close she had come to cancelling out on this date! What an effort it had been to climb into clothes that had been so horribly inappropriate for her mood!

She had to force a returning smile on her face and by the time she made it to the table, her jaw was aching and her nervous system was in overdrive.

She slipped into the chair facing him, barely aware of the waiter pulling it out for her, and placed her hand over her wine glass, asking instead for a glass of fresh juice.

'You look stunning.' Deep blue eyes roved appreciatively over her. 'I'm going to enjoy taking that dress off you in a couple of hours…'

'I'm…sorry I'm a little late,' Jennifer said weakly, fiddling with the end of the pashmina.

'Traffic!' He threw his hands up in a gesture of frustration at the horrors of getting around London. He was picking up something, an uneasy atmosphere, something he couldn't quite put his finger on.

'Actually, the traffic was fine. I just…left my house later than I expected…'

'Woman's prerogative.'

'I'm never late, James. I hate it.'

'Well, you're here now. At least you haven't bailed on me because your house mate was feeling down and needed a shoulder to cry on.'

Jennifer flushed. Little did he know that her occasional cancellations had been carefully orchestrated. A sense of self-preservation had made her instil a small amount of distance and she was very glad of that now.

She fiddled with her hair, made a few polite noises about the restaurant, told him that there was no need to bring her to such an expensive place, that she was more than happy with cheap and cheerful.

'I've never been out with a woman who hasn't appreciated being taken to somewhere grand.'

'I'm not impressed by what money can buy, James. How many times have I told you that?' She heard the sharp edge in her voice and she watched as he frowned and narrowed his deep blue eyes on her.

'Are we going to have an argument?' He sat back and folded his arms. 'I should warn you that I have no intention of participating.'

Now that he mentioned it, an argument was just what Jennifer wanted, something to release the sick tension that had been building over the past few hours. An argument would be a solid staging post for what had to follow.

'I'm not having an argument with you. I'm saying that I'm not impressed by...*all this*. I mean, it's just one of the things that reveal how different you and I are. Fundamentally.'

'Come again?' James sat forward and this time the navy eyes were sharp. 'I thought you would like to be treated to a meal out somewhere fancy. I hadn't realised that you see it as a direct attack on your moral code and I certainly hadn't thought that I would be accused of...what is it exactly? That you're accusing me of...?'

'I'm not accusing you of anything. I'm just saying that this isn't the sort of place I would choose to eat. Waiters bowing and scraping, food that doesn't look like food—'

'Fine. We'll leave.' He made to stand up and Jennifer tugged him back down.

'Don't be silly.'

'What's going on?'

'Nothing. Nothing's going on. Well...'

'Well...what?'

'I've been thinking...' She drew in a gulp of air and had to fight a sudden attack of giddiness. Did he have to look at her like that? As though he could see straight into her head? Her heart was beating fast, a painful drum roll that added to the vertigo.

'Never a good idea.' His unease was growing by the second. 'My advice to you? Don't think. Just enjoy.'

'You don't know what I've been thinking.'

'I don't need to know. I can see from your face that whatever it is, I won't want to hear.'

'I just want you to know that I stick to what I've said all along, James. You and I aren't suited. We have fun together but, in the long run, we're like oil and water. We just don't have personalities that blend together. I mean, not in the long term.' She stared down at the swirling patterns of her dress.

'I have no idea what you're talking about and if you're going to say something, then I suggest you actually look me in the face when you say it.'

'This…' She looked at him. 'All of this…has been fun, really great and I appreciated every second of it, but I think…I think it might be time we call it a day.'

'I'm not hearing this.' He kept his voice very low and very even. If he gave in to what he was feeling, he thought he might end up doing untold damage to the exquisite, mind-blowingly expensive decor in the restaurant. 'You're breaking up with me. Is that what you're saying?'

'In a manner of speaking.'

'What the hell does *that* mean? I don't know what's going on here, but this is not the place for this conversation. We're going back to my apartment.'

'No!' Jennifer could think of nothing worse. The familiarity…the kitchen where they had prepared meals together reminding her of how much she was going to lose…the coffee table where they had sat only a couple of days ago playing Scrabble…which she had brought from the house with her and which she had forced him to play as a relaxation technique, although that had gone through the window when he had decided that there were other, more enjoyable ways of relaxing…the bedroom with the king-sized bed, which she would no longer occupy…

It would all be too much.

James held up both hands in surrender but his eyes were cool and questioning when they rested on her face.

'Look.' She splayed her fingers on the table and stared intently at them. 'There's something I need to tell you but, first of all, we need to get this whole relationship straight.

We need to admit that it was never going to stay the course. We need to break up.'

James raked his fingers through his hair and found that his hands were shaking. 'Between last night and tonight, you've suddenly decided that we need to *break up*…and you expect me to *go along with you*? I'm not admitting anything of the sort.'

'This isn't how I meant this conversation to be, James. This isn't where I thought I'd find myself, but something's…something's cropped up…'

'What?' With something to focus on, his mind went into free fall. It was a weird sensation, a feeling of utterly and completely losing all self-control. 'You've found someone else. Is that it?' His voice was incredulous. Break up? How long had she been contemplating *that*? Had there been some other man lurking in the background? One of those fictitious sensitive, emotionally savvy guys she had once told him made ideal partner material? He could think of no other reason for her to be sitting opposite him now telling him that *it had been fun but*…

'Don't be crazy. I haven't found anyone else. When would I have had time to go out looking?'

'Are you telling me that you think I've monopolised your life? Is that it? Because I'm perfectly happy to take things at a slower pace.' He could scarcely credit the levels to which he was willing to accommodate her.

Jennifer was sure that he would be. He hadn't emotionally invested. He could always tame his rampant libido until such time as it was no longer rampant.

'No, it's not that.'

'Let me get this straight. For no particular reason, you've suddenly decided that we can't go on. There's no one else on the scene, we've both been having fun and yet it's no longer enough. Am I missing something here? Because it feels as if I am.'

'There's no easy way of telling you this, James, so I'm just going to come right out and say it. I'm pregnant.'

She couldn't look him in the face when she said it so she stared down at her lap instead while the silence thickened around them like treacle.

'You can't be. You're using contraception. I've seen that little packet of pills in the bathroom. Are you telling me that you've been pretending to take them?' At some point, the wires in his brain appeared to have disconnected. In possession of one huge, life-changing fact, he found that he could only fall back on the pointless details around it. 'I can't talk to you here, Jennifer.'

'I'm not going to your apartment.'

'Why the hell not?'

'Because I want to deal with this situation in neutral territory.'

'Your choice of words is astounding.'

'How *else* do you want me to phrase it, James? Shall I start by telling you that I'm sorry? Well, I *am*. And before you even *think* of accusing me of getting pregnant on purpose, then I'm warning you not to go there because that's the *very last thing on earth* I would do.'

'Message received loud and clear!'

'I *have* been on the pill. I can only think that that first time…'

'We used a condom. We were protected. We were *always* protected. This is madness. I can't believe I'm hearing any of this.'

'Because you signed up for a life you could control!'

'It's not going to get either of us anywhere if we start arguing with one another!'

'You're right,' Jennifer whispered. 'And I didn't come

here to argue with you. I'm happy to take the blame. The first time we made love, I used a condom that I'd had for absolutely ages...' *Four years to be precise. How ironic that the condom she had bought to enjoy sex with him all those years ago had become the condom that allowed her to fall pregnant.* 'It may have perished. They can.' Salt water seeping through the foil would do that, she thought, and if not salt water when her bag had dropped into the sea, then an infinitesimal puncture with the sharp edge of a key, or nail clipper or tweezers or any of the hundred and one items she had flung in her bag next to it over the years.

She had gone on the pill the second they had returned to London because he had laughed and told her that he would be a pauper at the rate they went through condoms, little knowing that by then it had been too late.

'I did go on the pill when we got back here so I never noticed that I hardly had any kind of period at all and nothing a couple of weeks ago, so I decided to go and see the doctor just to make sure that I was on the right dosage. Anyway—'

'You're pregnant.' It was finally sinking in. 'You're going to have a baby.'

'I'm sorry.' His face was ashen. 'You're in shock. You must be. I understand that and I'm sorry that I've spoilt the meal but it's been on my mind all day and I just wanted to get it out of the way. And now that I have, I think the sensible thing to do would be for me to leave and for you to take a little time out to adjust to the idea, so...'

He was going to be a father!

'But why didn't I notice?' he asked, dazed.

'We never notice things we aren't expecting. Not really. And I'm not one of those rake-thin types who show every ounce of weight they put on. Apparently someone with a fuller figure can hide a pregnancy for a lot longer.' Part of her wished that he would be open with his displeasure. Instead, he looked like someone who had been punched in the stomach and, instead of reacting, decided to lie on the ground and curl up instead. It wasn't him! That in itself was proof of how thrown he was and of course he would be! She had had a head start in the shock stakes. She had had several hours in which to absorb the news. The accusations would come when it really and truly sank in, the reality, the consequences, the potential to throw his neatly ordered life out of sync for ever. The waiter came and was waved away.

'You're going to have my baby and you greet me with the opening words that you want out of the relationship?'

'We don't *have* a relationship.' Jennifer tensed as she sensed the shift in the atmosphere. He had looked glazed but now his eyes were sharpening and focusing on her. 'We have…had…a passing physical interest in each other. And don't look at me like that. You know that I'm just being honest.' Was he aware of the fleeting pause she allowed, a window in which he could contradict her, tell her that things had changed, that he might not have entered their relationship with a future in mind but had found commitment along the way? The brief silence went unfilled. 'Neither of us counted on this,' she said abruptly.

'You're going to have my baby and the only way you can think of dealing with the problem is by breaking up…'

Jennifer stiffened at his use of the word *problem*.

'It seems the best solution,' she said coolly. 'You didn't ask for this to arise and I'm not going to punish you, or me for that matter, by putting you in a position of having to stand by me whether you like it or not.'

'I don't believe I'm hearing this. We're lovers but have you forgotten that we also happen to be friends?'

She had forgotten neither but how could she explain

that a baby needed more than a couple united by passion? Or even, for that matter, friendship?

'So tell me,' James said with increasing cool, 'how do you see this panning out? Perhaps you'd like me to walk away from you and leave you to get on with it?'

'If that's what you want to do, then I'll accept it.'

'If you really think that that would be an option I would consider, then you don't know me very well, do you?'

Which was why, of course, she had pre-empted any re-action by breaking up with him. She had known that he wouldn't walk away from the situation. She could never have fallen head over heels in love with a man capable of doing that, and that in itself was the problem. James would want involvement. He would want to do the right thing but his heart wouldn't be in it. Any affection he felt for her would eventually wither away under the strain of having to deal with a child he hadn't asked for and being stuck with a woman he had never envisaged as long term.

'We'll have to get married.' Something powerful stirred inside him, something he could scarcely identify.

'And that's exactly why I opened this conversation by telling you that it's over between us,' Jennifer said quietly. 'I know you want to do the right thing, but it wouldn't be fair on either of us to be shackled to each other for the sake of a child.'

They both broke off while the waiter came to take their orders. James didn't bother to consult the menu. He ordered fish and she followed suit, not caring what she ate. Her appetite had deserted her.

'And marriage!' She leaned forward to continue where she had left off. 'I bet you've never given a passing thought to the idea of getting married, have you?'

'That's not the point.'

'It's exactly the point,' Jennifer cried. 'Marriage is

something serious. A commitment between two people who see their lives united for ever.'

'At least that's the romantic interpretation of it.'

'What other interpretation could there possibly be?'

'Something more pragmatic. Think about it. One in every three marriages ends in the divorce courts and all of those bitter, sad, divorced couples probably sat across each other at a dinner table holding hands and waxing lyrical about growing old together.'

'But for two out of those three, the holding hands and waxing lyrical works. They end up together.'

'You're an eternal optimist. Experience has taught me to be a little more cautious. But none of that matters and we could argue about it for the remainder of the evening. The fact is, we're in a situation where there's no choice.'

Jennifer's heart sank. If she didn't love him, maybe it would have been easier to settle for the solution that made sense, but if she married him, she would be torn apart.

'I'm sorry, James,' she said shakily, 'but the answer has to be no. I can't marry you because you think it makes sense. When I get married, I want it to be for all the right reasons. I don't want to settle for a reluctant husband who would rather be with someone else but finds himself stuck with me. How healthy would that be for our child, anyway?'

How could life be suddenly turned on its head in the space of a few short hours? Very easily was the conclusion he was reaching as he looked at her stubborn, closed expression.

Rage at her blinding intransigence rushed through him in a tidal wave. 'And tell me this. How healthy would it be for our child to grow up without both parents there? Because that's something you need to consider! This isn't about you and your romantic notions of fairy-tale endings!'

Jennifer flinched and looked away. 'You're not going to make me change my mind,' she said, gathering all the strength at her disposal.

'No? Then let me provide you with an alternative scenario. Our child grows up in a split family and in due course finds out that both of us could have been there but you wouldn't have it because you were determined to look for Mr Right, who may or may not come along. And if he does coming along…well, I'm telling you right now that he won't be involved in bringing up my child because I'll fight for custody.'

Battle lines had been drawn but Jennifer could scarcely think so far ahead.

'And your father. What do you intend to tell *him*?' This before she had had time to digest his previous statement.

'I haven't thought—'

'Because don't even think about insinuating to your father that I haven't offered to do the decent thing. I intend to make it perfectly clear to my mother and to John that I've proposed to you and that you have in your wisdom decided that the best course of action is to go it alone. We can see what they make of that.'

'I don't want to fall out over this—'

'Then maybe you should have thought about broaching this bombshell in a slightly different way!'

'It wouldn't have made any difference. The result would have been the same and I'm sorry about that. Look, I can't eat any more. I've lost my appetite. I think I should go back home now.' She half stood, swayed and sat back down. In an instant, James was at her side, all thoughts of pursuing his argument forgotten.

Jennifer was barely aware of him settling the bill, leaving a more than generous tip for the waiter, who had sensed an atmosphere and had patiently left them alone. She had her head in her hands.

'Honestly, I'm fine, James,' she protested weakly as soon as they were out of the restaurant.

'How long have these giddy spells been going on?'

'I get them now and again. It's nothing to worry about…' But it was comforting to have his arms around her, supporting her as he hailed a black cab and settled her inside as though she were a piece of porcelain.

'What did the doctor say?'

'I didn't mention them. I was too shocked at finding out I was pregnant!'

'You should go back. Have a complete check-up. What's with these people? Don't they know how to do their jobs?'

'Don't worry. It's nothing!'

For the first time since finding out about the pregnancy, she wondered whether she was making the right decision in turning down his proposal. Whether he loved her or not, he was a source of strength and when would she need that strength more than right now? When she was facing motherhood? He wanted to do the right thing. Was it selfish of her to hold tight to her principles? Or in the big scheme of things, was *he* right? Could his suggestion of a loveless marriage be the right one?

The questions churned around in her head for the duration of the trip back to her house although by the time they got there, the giddiness had disappeared, replaced by utter exhaustion.

'We can talk about this tomorrow,' she told him by the front door and James looked at her in glowering frustration, his hands jammed into his pockets.

'We weren't talking back there. You were dictating terms and I was supposed to listen and obey.'

'It's hard for me too, James, but marriage is a big deal

for me and I want to marry a guy who wants me in his life for all the right reasons.'

'Weren't you happy when we were together?' he asked gruffly and, taken aback by the directness of the question, Jennifer nodded.

'So now that there's a baby, why would that change?'

'Because,' Jennifer said helplessly, 'it's not just about having lots of sex until it fizzles out and we say goodbye to one another and move on.'

'But the having lots of sex is a start.'

'You're so physical, James.' She could feel her body quivering at the hundreds of memories she had of them making love. She would never forget a single one of them. 'The cab driver's going to start getting impatient.'

'Why? It's good money sitting there with the meter running. We still need to talk this one through. In fact, let me get rid of him. I could come in with you. The lights are all off, which means your house mate probably isn't here. We could discuss this in private...'

What he meant was that they would make love. It was the language he spoke most fluently and she knew she couldn't trust herself if they climbed into bed together.

'We both need to think about this.' She placed her hand on his chest to stop him from following her into the house. 'Tomorrow we'll think about the practicalities. And by the way, I would never tell Dad that you weren't taking the responsible attitude, James,' she returned to the insinuation she had never protested.

He nodded, at a loss for anything else to say. What did she mean about right reasons? Wasn't a child a good enough reason for them to be married? It wasn't as though they didn't get along, weren't fantastically suited in bed. He was genuinely bewildered at his failure to convince her.

He wondered whether he should have taken a step back,

led up gently to the notion of getting married. She had stated from the very beginning that she wasn't looking for commitment and yet he had jumped in, feet first, arrogantly assuming that she would fall in line with what he wanted. But how could she fail to see that getting married was the most practical solution to the situation? And what about *them*? Was what they had about to dissolve because a baby on the way had crystallised the fact that she didn't see him as a long-term partner? He felt hollow and angry and impotent.

At any rate, there was nothing to be gained by continuing to push her into the decision he wanted her to take. It was clear that she wasn't about to let him into the house and she looked utterly shattered. For her own good, he knew that he should go and let her get some rest, but he still hesitated because he couldn't think of her walking away from him. It wasn't going to happen. He would make sure of that.

His mind returned to that picture-perfect house, bristling with new furniture, updated to within an inch of its life, perched in its very own garden, a stone's throw from all those quaint village services she had always raved about. He had intended to present it to her with casual indifference, a little something he had pulled out of his portfolio. He would have offered it to her at a laughably low rental and suggested that it would hit the open market if she decided not to take it because of her pride. Faced with that, he had known that she would not have been able to resist.

Well, the house was still there but now it would be his trump card.

The sick feeling of helplessness that had earlier gripped him began to dissipate. He was a man who thought quickly and made decisions at the speed of light. He was a man who found solutions. He had extended the obvious solution and had been knocked back, but now he had another solution up his sleeve and thank God for that. For a few minutes back there, he had not been able to think clearly.

'You're right,' he said heavily. 'Although I don't like leaving you like this. You look as though you're about to collapse.'

'It's been a long day.' For one craven, cowardly moment Jennifer was tempted to open the door for him, let him in so that she could curl up in his arms and fall asleep. She just wanted to hold him close because he made her feel safe.

'Tomorrow, then,' he murmured, badly wanting to touch her but instead pushing himself away from the doorframe. 'If you still want to meet on neutral territory, then we will. If you're agreeable to coming to my apartment, I will get my caterer to prepare something. We can talk about what happens next…take it from there…'

CHAPTER EIGHT

TAKE it from there...yes. Discuss the practicalities...of course. But are you excited...even just a little...?

That was the question Jennifer would really have liked to have asked him. Once she had recovered from the shock of being told that she was pregnant, she had been thrilled at the thought of having a baby, of having *James's* baby. In the space of twenty-four hours, she had managed to wonder what the baby would look like, what sex it would be, whether he or she would attend a single-sex school or a mixed one, what career path he or she would follow, what his or her girlfriends or boyfriends would do for a living and at what age he or she would be married.

She was *excited*.

She didn't think that excitement would feature on James's chart of possible reactions to the news. She thought that the best she could hope for would maybe be *acceptance* and its close relation, *resignation*.

How could he not see that any marriage based on a situation where those two damning words were involved would never be anything more than a marriage of convenience? Destined to eventually fail because the last thing a marriage should ever be was *convenient*?

Nevertheless, that didn't stop Jennifer wondering what it would be like to be married to him. She marvelled, sitting in the back of the chauffeur-driven car he had sent for her, how close she could be to everything she had ever dared hope for while still being so far. She wondered whether his anger and disappointment at what had happened would have gathered steam overnight. Had he lain awake thinking that, thanks to her idiocy, his plans for his life were now lying in ruins at his feet? Without a roomful of unwitting chaperones to keep the full extent of his reactions at bay, would he feel free in the privacy of his own apartment to really let rip when she showed up?

At any rate, they were going to have to reach some sort of agreement with regards to the way forward because she couldn't keep her father in the dark for ever. She was due to visit the following weekend and she intended to break the news then that he would be a grandfather.

With the days getting longer, it was still bright by the time she got to his apartment at a little after six and there was no time to brace herself for the sight of him because he was waiting for her in the marbled foyer as she entered. Fresh from work and still in his suit, although without a jacket and with the sleeves of his white shirt rolled to his elbows and his tie loosely pulled down to allow the top two buttons of his shirt to be undone.

'Oh.' Jennifer came to a dead stop as she was buzzed in. 'Have you just arrived from work? You should have called and asked me to get here a bit later. I wouldn't have minded.' All over again, she felt that powerful sensual tug towards him, as though her body had a will of its own the second she was in his presence.

James frowned. He had grown accustomed to her exuberance. Her awkward formality was a jarring reminder of the situation in which they had now found themselves. He shoved his hands in his pockets and took a few seconds to look at her. She was wearing a stretchy knee-length dress in shades of green and was it his imagination or could he now see evidence of her pregnancy? More rounded curves, breasts that would be substantially bigger than a handful… On cue, he felt himself harden and, given the inappropriateness of the moment, he dealt with that by walking towards her and keeping his eyes firmly focused on her face.

'Don't worry about it. Plans have changed. We won't be heading up to the apartment.'

'Where are we going?'

'Should you be wearing such tight dresses?' He cupped her elbow with his hand and hustled her back towards the front door. 'Now that you're pregnant?' Hell, she looked even sexier than ever. What man wouldn't run into a lamp post trying to catch a backward glance at her luscious body. 'Your breasts are spilling out of the top of that dress!'

'Yes, I've put on some weight.' Jennifer felt herself flush at the thought that he might be turned off at the sight of her increasing size. He was, after all, a man who was primarily concerned with the whole 'body beautiful' rubbish. If he wanted her to hide herself in smocks now, then what on earth was he going to do when she reached the size of a barrage balloon?

'I don't need to get into maternity frocks just yet,' she snapped, watching as the chauffeur hurried to open the passenger door for her. 'Some women *never* buy maternity clothes! Have you seen how unappealing they can be?'

'You won't be one of those women.' He grimaced in distaste at the memory of a certain recent magazine cover that had been lying around his apartment, courtesy of Jennifer. It had featured a semi naked actress, heavily pregnant, in a few shreds of clothing that had done nothing to conceal her enormous belly.

'You can't tell me what I can or can't wear!'

'I just have. Tomorrow we'll go shopping. Get you some looser stuff.'

'Is that one of the *practicalities* you were planning on talking to me about?' She spun to face him as soon as the passenger door had slammed behind him. 'Because if it was, then you can consider it discussed and struck off the list!'

James gritted his teeth in frustration. Not the perfect start to the evening.

In the ensuing silence, Jennifer debated whether she should apologise for overreacting and decided firmly against it.

'Where are we going?' she asked eventually.

'There's something I'd like to show you.'

'Really? But I thought we were going to discuss…how we're going to deal with the situation…'

'Consider what I show you as part of the ongoing conversation on the subject. Were you all right when you got back to your place last night?'

'What do you mean?'

'You felt faint at the restaurant.'

'Oh, yes. Well, that was just my nerves.' She rested her head against the window and looked at him from under her lashes. 'I know you think that I'm being unreasonable, James…'

'This is a debate that can only end up going round in circles, Jennifer. Let's put it on the back burner for the moment and concentrate on a more productive way forward, shall we?' They had cleared the centre of London in record time and were now heading south west. 'Question— when do you intend to break the news to John? I'd like to be there.'

'I don't see why—'

'Is every suggestion I make going to end in a point-less argument?'

'I'm sorry. I don't mean to be difficult.'

'Good. At least we agree on one thing. It's a start!'

'There's no need to be sarcastic, James. I'm trying my best.' She looked away quickly. Honesty forced her to admit to herself that that was hardly the strict truth. So far he had risen admirably to the occasion and she had relentlessly shot him down in flames. Was it his fault that he couldn't supply her with the words that she wanted to hear? He had not once apportioned any blame on her shoulders, even though he must surely be blaming her in his head. He had offered to do the decent thing and was probably baffled by her refusal to even consider the possibility of marriage. He had no intention of leaving her in the lurch even though he doubtless wanted to run as far as his feet could take him to the farthest corner of the earth because fatherhood, for the man who couldn't commit, would have been the final albatross around his neck. His *one hundred per cent innocent* neck.

He wanted to do what was best for the baby growing inside her, *their baby*, and all she could think was that he didn't love her, that she would become a burden, that he would end up hating her. He was thinking of the baby. She, on the other hand, was thinking about herself.

Consumed by a sudden attack of guilt, Jennifer lapsed into nervous silence and watched as they cleared through the busiest part of London, heading out until increasing patches of greenery replaced the unremitting grey of pavements and roads.

She still had no idea where they were heading and was surprised when, eventually, the car weaved through a series of small streets, emerging in front of a house that looked as though it had leapt out of a story book.

'Where are we?' She looked at him with bewilderment and James offered her a ghost of a smile.

Thirty-six hours ago, he thought, this would have been a terrific surprise for her. Now, it was part of his back-up plan.

'We're in one of the leafier parts of London.'

'I didn't think they existed. At least, not like this...' She couldn't take her eyes off the picture-perfect house in front of her. The small front garden was a riot of flowers on the verge of bursting into summer colour. A path led to the front door of the house, which was small but exqui-site. A child's painting of a house, perfectly proportioned with massive bay windows on the ground floor, flanking a black door, a chimney minus the smoke, beautiful aged stone awash with wisteria. To one side was a garage and to the other one mature tree, behind which peeped a lawn swerving away towards the back of the house.

'Who lives here?' she asked suspiciously. 'If you had told me that we would be visiting friends of yours, then I might have worn something different.' She was annoyed to discover that she was already thinking about chang-ing her wardrobe, stocking it with baggier, more shape-less garments even though she had protested otherwise.

'It's one of the properties in my private portfolio.' He was already unlocking the front door, pushing it open and standing aside to let her brush past him.

'You never mentioned this!'

'I never saw the need.'

'It's wonderful, James.' Flagstones in the hallway, cream walls recently painted from the looks of it, a deep burnished wooden banister leading up to the first floor. Jennifer tentatively took a few steps forward and then, be-coming braver, began exploring the house. It was much bigger on the inside than it looked from the outside.

Downstairs, a range of rooms radiated from the central hallway. There was a small but comfortable sitting room, a dining room, a box room with built in shelves and cupboards that had clearly been used as an office, a separate television room and, of course, the kitchen, which had been extended so that it was easily big enough to fit a generous-sized table as well as furniture. It was a kitchen and conservatory without the division of walls. French doors led out to a perfectly landscaped garden. Whoever had owned the house previously had been a keen gardener with an eye for detail. Various fruit trees lined the perimeter of the garden and between them nestled a bench from which you could look back towards the house and appreciate the abundance of plants and flowers.

'Gosh.' Eyes gleaming, Jennifer turned back to James. 'I can't believe you would ever choose to live where you do when this place could have been an option.'

'It's very country cottage. Why don't you come and see the upstairs? I think you'll like the four-poster bed in the master bedroom. Everything has been done to the highest possible standard while maintaining the period of the place. Did you get a chance to see the Aga in the kitchen? I can't think that there would be many properties in London boasting one of those.' He wondered what on earth someone would do with one of those. He had no idea. It looked like a baffling piece of kitchen equipment, but she had wistfully mentioned them in the past and he had taken mental note. In fact, he had furnished the house with her in mind. He had been surprised at how many details of her likes and dislikes he had gathered and stored over time.

'You sound like an estate agent.' But for the first time since she had broken the news, James could see laughter in her eyes. Where he had failed, the house appeared to be succeeding, and before she could remember that she was fighting him he ushered her up the stairs so that she could gasp and admire the bedrooms, the bathrooms, the walk-in dressing room in the master bedroom.

'So,' he said, once they had returned to the kitchen and taken up position at the wooden kitchen table, wooden because she had previously expressed a dislike for all things chrome and glass, 'what do you think of the place?'

'You know what I think, James. I imagine it's been written all over my face.'

'Good. Because this is one of the practicalities I want to talk to you about. A shared house isn't going to be suitable for a baby. This, on the other hand...' He made a sweeping gesture to encompass the cottage while keeping his deep blue eyes firmly fixed on her face.

He could see the indecision on her face and had to fight down the desire to tell her that she had no choice in the matter. Laying down laws and trying to browbeat her into submission hadn't worked. 'I firmly believe,' he carried on smoothly, just as she was about to say something, 'that children benefit from a more relaxed lifestyle than living in the centre of London can provide for them. Don't you remember how much fun it was for you growing up in the countryside? Granted this is nothing like the countryside but there's a garden, quite a big one by London standards, and all the shops you might need are within walking distance.'

'But don't you have plans for this place? I mean, was it rented out before? I hope you didn't turf out any tenants, James.'

'Your faith in me knows no bounds,' he said drily, knowing that part one of the battle had been won. 'I didn't turf anyone out. You like the place and I think it would be ideal. It's within commuting distance from London. In fact, surprisingly convenient for the underground...which brings me to the small matter of your job.' Which, he could see from the expression on her face, was something she had given no thought to.

'My job…I hadn't really thought…'

'It's going to be awkward.'

'Are you telling me that I'm out of a job?' Jennifer demanded, bristling.

'Far be it from me to tell you anything of the sort. But think about it. You're pregnant. You won't be able to keep it under wraps and sooner or later it's going to emerge that I'm the father. Might not be the most comfortable situation in the world for you…'

'So I leave and do what?'

'Practicality number two. Money. Naturally, if you want to stay on at the company then there's no way I would stand in your way. I have no problem dealing with whispers behind my back and if you think you can deal with that as well, then I'll support you one hundred per cent in staying on.' He allowed a few seconds of silence to follow that statement. It took a strong person to survive the toxicity of office politics. 'At any rate, whether you continue working or not, I intend to open a bank account for you and, just in case you want to argue with me over this, I'm telling you right now that no child of mine will want for anything because you're too proud to accept money from me.'

'I have no objection to you paying for our child, James,' Jennifer muttered awkwardly as she feverishly played in her mind the scenario of her co-workers gossiping behind her back. She could be a genius at her job and would still not be able to fight the rumours that she had got where she was because she had been sleeping with her boss. Pregnant by him would stoke the fires from a slow simmer to a blazing inferno.

'*You* come as part of the deal, Jen,' James said gently. 'I intend to ensure that your bank balance allows you freedom to choose what you want to do. Carry on working for the company, go ahead. Find another job closer to this place, then feel free. Give up work altogether, then I'm one hundred per cent happy with that solution. It's up to you. Of course...' he appeared to mull over his next few words '...I'm jumping the gun here, assuming that you don't have a problem moving out here...'

'It might be better all round to be out of central London,' Jennifer concurred, trying hard not to show her relief at leaving the house. Ellie was free, single and disengaged. She played loud music and entertained her boyfriends with exuberance. It was her house. In between all the other stresses, Jennifer had wondered how a baby would feature in that set-up. She sneaked a glance at the super modern kitchen, the granite work surfaces, which blended so harmoniously with the old-fashioned dresser and the mellow kitchen table with mismatched, charming chairs. She could get a kitten.

'And the job?'

'I'll have to think about that.'

'But not for too long, I hope. Your replacement would have to be found,' he murmured. 'Could take ages...but moving on from there to the thorny subject of our parents...'

'I told you...I'm going to break it to Dad on the weekend.'

'I'd also like my mother to be present...'

'Yes. Of course.' She hadn't actually dwelled on that particular horror waiting round the corner, but, of course, Daisy would have to be present.

'How do you think they're going to take the news?'

'Why are you talking about this,' she said with a hint of desperation. 'I'm just living one day at a time.'

'Which doesn't mean that tomorrow isn't going to come.'

'I know *that*.'

'Do you?'

'Of course I do! I'm not a complete idiot. I know there are going to be lots of complications to sort out along the way but at least we've managed to do something about the first one. I mean, I *had* actually wondered whether sharing Ellie's house was going to be suitable for a baby. And it's a busy road. I've always felt sorry for those women pushing buggies on crowded streets, trying to get them on and off the buses…'

'The cottage is vacant. I'll make sure that you're moved by the end of next week. You won't have to lift a finger.'

Hearing him say that was like heaven to her ears. She didn't want to feel burdensome to a man who didn't love her, but, still, she could feel his strength seep into her and the temptation to close her eyes and lean on him was so great that she felt giddy.

James stood up, walked to the fridge and told her that he had taken the liberty of getting his caterers to prepare a light supper for them.

'Sit,' he ordered, when she automatically began rising to her feet. 'I've got this.'

'I feel like I'm on a roller-coaster ride with someone else manning the controls,' Jennifer mumbled, but half-heartedly, and he glanced across at her with a crooked smile.

'Go with it.'

'But I don't want you to feel that you've got to play the responsible role,' she protested, clinging to her principles by the tips of her fingers. 'You haven't listened to what

I've said. You don't have to *take care of me*. It's enough that you're allowing me to move to this cottage.'

'And you haven't listened to *me*. I intend to be fully involved. I have no intention of letting you play the independent woman, keeping me at a distance while you wait for Mr Right to come along.' Just thinking about that set his teeth on edge. Food ready, James took it to the table in its original containers, which he had stuck in the microwave, and placed two plates and cutlery alongside them.

'We have to get past this…atmosphere…' he gritted, sitting back and waiting as she dished out some of the one-pot dinner for herself. He had had a little time to think about the change in her attitude towards him and he had worked out the reason behind it. Where their relationship had always been one of easy-going friendship, which had developed into something even more so after they had become lovers, the fact of her unexpected pregnancy had thrown up all the downsides to what they had. She could no longer relax with him because she now felt trapped, hemmed in by a situation she couldn't reverse and, in one way or another, stuck with someone she had always planned on moving away from eventually. She wasn't in it through free choice. She was in it through lack of option.

Which didn't mean that he was going to allow himself to be shunted aside so that she could start her search for her knight in shining armour the second their baby was born. No way.

Which, in turn, brought him to the delicate part of the proceedings.

He thoughtfully worked his way through the meal in front of him, half listening as she tried to assure him that there was *no atmosphere*, that she was *just tense, that's all*, that she was very pleased that they were both being *so adult* about everything. In mid-sentence, he cut her short by raising his hand, and Jennifer stuttered to silence.

'Why don't we go and relax in the sitting room?'

'It feels odd…when someone's probably just left this place…'

'Let me dispel that myth,' he drawled, getting to his feet. 'The house was last rented out over ten months ago. It's just been recently refurbished.'

'Has it? Why? Were you going to put it on for rental again?'

James flushed darkly. 'It doesn't matter.'

'So…all this furniture is new?' Jennifer stood up, marvelling that there was not a single thing in the house that she wouldn't have chosen herself.

'Yes, I had my people equip it,' he allowed, omitting the fact that he had personally instructed them in what to buy.

'They couldn't have chosen better.' Jennifer gazed admiringly at the deep, plush sofa in the sitting room, the broad comfortable chairs on either side of it. Every detail took her breath away, from the rich burgundy drapes to the intricate Persian rug covering the polished wooden floor.

She flopped onto the sofa and curled her legs under her. Disturbingly, because she was determined to keep her distance, James sat next to her, then turned, his arms along the back of the sofa and behind her.

'So…'

'So…?' She could feel her heartbeat pick up and a fine film of perspiration break out over her body.

'So I want you to tell me why the atmosphere has changed so fast between us…'

'Well, isn't it obvious?' Jennifer stammered. She blinked rapidly to try and stabilise her nerves, which were suddenly in wild free fall. Two days ago, she would have been in his arms right now, two days ago they would have been making love. Yes, things had changed, but he would still be bemused by her retreat. Without the complication of being emotionally involved, lust, for him, would still be intact.

'Nope.' He inclined his head and continued staring at her.

Jennifer wished that she had some sharp retort to counter that, but she didn't. She was suddenly hot and bothered and flustered and very much aware of his proximity.

'Then it should be…'

'Why is that?' He sighed and raked his fingers through his hair in a gesture that was so familiar that Jennifer felt her heart tug painfully. 'Has pregnancy done something to your hormones? Turned you off sex? Or have you suddenly found that you're no longer attracted to me because you're carrying my baby?'

'No!' The hot denial was out before she had time to think about it and swallow the shaming truth back down. 'I mean…'

'You mean you *are* still attracted to me,' James murmured with satisfaction.

'That's not the point!'

'The point being?'

'The point being that there's more at stake than just the two of us being attracted to each other and *having fun*, no *strings attached*.'

'You say *having fun* as though it's a crime against humanity.'

'Stop confusing me,' Jennifer cried, standing up agitatedly and pacing the sitting room, aware of his deep blue eyes thoughtfully following her. She paused to stand in front of him. She was fired up with a tangle of confusing emotions. She could barely think properly. She wasn't expecting him to reach out and place his hand gently on her stomach. She froze.

'I want to feel it,' James said unevenly. Children had never appeared on his radar but now that he knew that she was carrying his child, he was driven to have tangible evidence of it, wanted to feel the more rounded stomach.

'When will you feel it moving?'

'James, please…'

'I took part in the creation…surely you wouldn't deny me the chance to feel it?' He slipped his hands under her dress and gently tugged it up to expose her stomach. He felt her release her breath on a shudder but she didn't move away. How oblivious had he been? She was by no means big but she was certainly bigger than when they had first become lovers, her stomach smooth and firm but no longer flat. She was wearing little cotton briefs and they were low enough for him to see the shadow of soft, downy hair peeping above the elastic band.

He closed his eyes, faint with an overwhelming surge of intense, driven craving. It was like nothing he had ever felt in his life before. He had had friends who had wittered interminably about the joys of parenthood, who had reliably informed him that having a baby was like nothing on earth. He had always listened politely and promptly shoved the rhapsodies into the waste disposal unit in his head. Now, he wondered…was this what it was all about? This weird feeling that left him shaken and uncharacteristically out of control?

He would savour the moment and not question its origin. He felt her fingers settle into his hair as he shoved the dress farther up so that her bra was just visible.

With a soft tug he pulled her towards him onto the sofa and she fell with a little thud into the squashy cushions.

Jennifer knew that this was not how the evening was

supposed to proceed. She was *vulnerable* and should be *protecting herself.* That certainly did not include letting him pull her dress over her head, which he was now doing, not to mention unhook her bra so that he could ease it off her shoulders to expose breasts that were sensitive and tingling with wanting him to touch them.

Which, of course, he did, but not until he had told her how her body had changed.

He grazed his teeth against her nipples, sending a compulsive shiver rippling through her body. 'How couldn't I have seen the changes to your body?'

'You weren't looking,' Jennifer breathed unevenly. 'Nor was I and, like I've said, we just don't really notice what we're not expecting.' In fact, she had known that she had put on weight, but she had assumed that it was because she had been eating more, enjoying the domestic life with a man who refused to be tamed.

James barely heard her. He was too busy licking and tasting her, circling the stiff buds with his tongue before lavishing his attention on them in turn. She arched up, eyes closed, with her hands clasped behind her back.

His mouth was clamped on one nipple and as he sucked it she twisted and moaned, automatically parting her legs, inviting his hand to cup the throbbing mound between her thighs.

He could feel her dampness seeping through the cotton underwear but he was in no hurry to take off the flimsy garment. Instead, he pressed down and kept up the insistent pressure as he continued to lose himself in her glorious breasts. He liked the way she writhed every time he dipped his fingers deeper into her wetness. How could she hold herself at a distance from him? How could she deny that what they had together was good? Beyond good? He slipped his hand underneath the briefs and she groaned as his searching fingers began stroking her, over and over and over again, rubbing her clitoris until she wanted to pass out with pleasure.

They made love slowly, as though they had all the time in the world, and afterwards she almost dozed off in his arms.

'We shouldn't have done that,' was what she said instead, hating herself for having succumbed and terrified that it would just be the start of a pattern. He would get too close and she would give in because she was weak. She scrambled to push herself away from him but he yanked her back.

'Try and say that with conviction and I might start believing you.'

'I mean it, James. It's not on.'

'That's not what your body spent the past hour telling me.'

'And I don't *want* to let *my body* deal with this situation!' She pushed against him and scrambled around for her clothes, ashamed of herself.

James propped himself up and looked at her as she wriggled into the dress.

'I know you don't,' he agreed gravely, and Jennifer shot him a suspicious look from under her lashes.

'You do?' She looked at him uncertainly.

James sat up, strolled to where his boxers had been tossed, put them on and then turned to look at her.

'You're still attracted to me but you don't want that to get in the way of making what you think is the right decision.'

'Well…yes.' She sat back down, although this time on one of the chairs instead of on the sofa. Her body was as stiff as board and her hands rested primly on her knees as she continued to warily look at him. Fading light made his half-clothed body look as sculpted and as perfect as a classical Greek statue. She thought it would help if he could stick a shirt on.

'And I apologise unreservedly if I took advantage of your weakness and seduced you.'

'Well, you're not entirely to blame...' Jennifer was driven to admit, looking away with a guilty flush.

'Of course you're not going to want to get back into the situation we had, given the circumstances.'

'No-o-o...' Jennifer dragged out that one syllable for as long as she could while she tried to figure out where his speech was going.

'In a matter like this, you simply don't see the value of thinking with your head.'

'It's not *that*—'

'And I won't waste time trying to make you see that this is *just* the time when you *should* be thinking with your head. You don't want to marry me and I accept that.'

'Really? You do?' Why did that hurt so much?

'Why do you sound so surprised?'

'Because you seemed so convinced that getting married was the only option we had. As if we were still living in Victorian times and you had to make an honest woman of me, however unhappy we might both have ended up being!'

James held his cool and continued to look steadily at her. 'Let's just say that I'm willing to make compromises in that area.'

'What sort of compromises?'

'You move in here and I move in with you. No marriage, but I think we should see how it works out, give this a chance for the sake of the baby. If it doesn't work out, then we do the modern thing and walk away from each other.' He flushed darkly and looked away. 'We were happy…before this all blew up,' he said in a rough undertone. 'What's to say that we couldn't be happy again?'

CHAPTER NINE

JAMES didn't realise just how happy life with Jennifer was until he got her panicked call in the middle of a meeting.

When he had suggested that they live together, he had had no idea what he had been letting himself in for. He was a man accustomed to freedom of movement and independence, fundamentally unanswerable to anyone. Of course, he acknowledged that that state of affairs had undergone some change in the weeks after they had become lovers. He had also acknowledged that had she agreed to his original terms they would probably have been married by now, but somehow the fact of marriage had seemed less daunting than the fact of living together.

With a sense of duty no longer in the equation, living together had struck him as more of a commitment, even though he couldn't fathom why.

He had engineered a smooth transition for her from apartment to house. Despite her reassurances that she was as healthy as a horse, waving aside the occasional giddy spell as nothing to worry about, insisting that she continue working until a suitable replacement was found for her position, he made sure that she had as little to do as humanly possible during the actual move. Packing a few personal items into a suitcase was just about all he allowed her to get away with.

Clearing his own apartment had been a far weirder experience. The enormity of what he was doing only struck him when, after two days and a lot of overtime from engineers kitting out an office space in the house, he finally closed the front door on the outside world and joined her in the kitchen for their first meal as…a couple living together.

It had felt like a massive step but he had made sure to conceal any trepidation from her. He knew that she remained wary and hesitant and pregnancy appeared to have made her unpredictable. It happened. He knew. He had surreptitiously bought a pregnancy book and had read it cover to cover. He now felt equipped to start his own advice column.

'James…do you think you could get here?'

'What's wrong?' Few people had his private cell number. He had felt his phone vibrate in his pocket and her name had popped up. Immediately he had silently indicated to the assembled financiers that they should continue with the meeting and he had left the conference room. When she had started working at the little publishing company that he had inherited as part of the much bigger takeover package, Jennifer had never contacted him. She had quit two weeks previously and not once had she called him at work, even though he had repeatedly told her that she was more than welcome to interrupt his working day.

If the tone of her voice hadn't alerted him that something was wrong, the mere fact that she had called would have.

An emotion shifted into gear that he almost couldn't recognise. It was fear.

'I'm bleeding…I'm sure there's nothing to worry about—'

'I'm on my way.'

Jennifer lay back on the sofa with her legs raised and

tried to stay calm. Looking around her, she took in all the small touches she had introduced to the house that had very quickly felt like a home. The vases filled with flowers picked from the garden, the framed photos on the mantelpiece, the ornaments she had picked up from Portobello Market a couple of weekends previously. She wasn't entirely certain that James even noticed them and she hadn't wanted to point them out.

She had been gutted when all talk of marriage had been dropped so quickly. Had he been relieved that that final act of commitment had been avoided? Living together was so different and, of course, she had no one but herself to blame for not grabbing his marriage proposal when it had been on the cards.

Not that she regretted it. She still believed that without love a marriage was nothing more than a sham and yet…

Hadn't he been just the perfect partner ever since they had moved in together? She constantly told him that there was no need for him to treat her as though she could break at any given moment, and yet hadn't she loved every minute of it? Hadn't she begun to hope that the love he didn't feel for her might begin to grow from affection?

And now…

Jennifer didn't want to think that she might lose this baby. She wished that she had paid more attention to those dizzy spells she had been having off and on. If she lost the baby, then what would happen to her and James? It was a question she didn't want to think about because the answer was too agonising to deal with.

She closed her eyes and kept as still as possible but her mind continued to freewheel inside her head, irrespective of her desperation to keep it under control. She had already invested so much love into this unborn baby. How would she cope if anything happened?

She sagged with blessed relief as she heard the sound of James's key being inserted into the door, and he was in the act of removing his jacket as he pushed open the sitting room door and strode towards her, his face grey with worry.

'I shouldn't have bothered you—' She smiled weakly as he snapped out his mobile and began dialling.

'And hurry!'

'Who have you called?'

'The doctor.'

'I panicked. I'm sorry, James. I'm sure all I need is a bit of rest.'

James knelt down next to her and slipped her hand into his. 'You're not a doctor, Jen. You don't know what you need. Gregory is the top guy in London and a personal friend of the family. I asked him whether I should get an ambulance to take you to hospital but he said that he'll give you the once-over first. You scared the hell out of me.'

'I didn't mean to.'

He asked her about her symptoms, detailed questions to which he produced a series of clinical answers, and she smiled when he confessed to the pregnancy book languishing in his briefcase.

'A little knowledge is a dangerous thing, James.'

'Why didn't you tell me sooner that the giddy spells hadn't stopped?'

'I didn't want to worry you. I didn't think that there was anything to worry about…' And besides, she could have added truthfully, she hadn't wanted to rock the boat. She hadn't wanted to face up to anything that might cast a shadow over the picture-perfect life they had been living for the past few weeks. Except uncomfortable questions couldn't be put to bed by ignoring them and they were out of the box now, demanding attention.

'I know you're going to tell me that this isn't the right time to have this conversation, James, but—'

'It's the right time.'

Jennifer's eyes fluttered and she felt her heartbeat quicken.

'You don't know what I'm going to say...'

'I do.' He smiled crookedly at her. 'Do you think I don't know you a bit by now? Whenever you want to broach a delicate topic of conversation, you lick your lips for courage and begin to play with your hair.'

'I didn't think you noticed stuff like that.'

'You'd be surprised what I notice.' *About you.* 'You won't lose this baby.'

'You can't say that and what if I do?' There. It was out. She closed her eyes and calmed herself by taking deep breaths. Deliberately, she stuck her hands by her sides and fidgeted with the baggy tee shirt she was wearing.

'Then the time is right for us to talk about what happens. Before Gregory gets here. Stress isn't good for you and I don't want to stress you out but I need to say something.'

Jennifer looked at him with resignation. She wanted to put her hand over his mouth and hold the words back but he was right. He needed to tell her that their arrangement would not survive a miscarriage. The stress of hearing it would be a great deal less than the stress of lying here pretending that everything was just fine. And if she didn't lose the baby, then it would be good to know the next step forward. She realised that through the happiness and joy of the past few weeks, there had remained a poisonous thread of doubt that things would continue the way they were for ever more. That just wasn't how life worked. Now, he would put a face to those doubtful shadows and, yes, there would be disappointment all round, because their respective parents had accepted the situation and given their full support, but life was full of disappointment, wasn't it?

'I know that sharing this house with me probably wasn't what you had in mind when you realised that you were pregnant. You were only just coming into your own and suddenly…fate decides that it's time for you to have another learning curve…'

'What do you mean *coming into my own*?'

'I mean—' he sighed heavily and raked his fingers through his hair '—you'd led a sheltered life and then you go to Paris and return a changed person. You're sexy as hell and you're on a journey of discovery.'

'I hadn't realised that I was that adventurous.'

'You fell into a relationship with me to fulfil some youthful infatuation but I know you still want to get out there and discover what the world has in store for you.'

'I do?'

'Of course you do. You said as much when you told me that I was unfinished business. Unfinished business comes to an end eventually.' He looked away, his broodingly handsome face flushed. 'I guess I maybe ambushed you when I suggested we live together… You'd already turned down my marriage proposal. I'll admit that there was a certain amount of blackmail involved when I suggested that we live together. How could you turn down marriage *and* turn down the other reasonable alternative on the table without appearing utterly selfish?' He threw her a challenging look.

'It was a good idea,' Jennifer murmured, heart beating fast.

'And it *has* been…hasn't it? Good?'

Jennifer nodded, because it required too much effort to try and work out how much of herself she should give away. Should she tell him that it couldn't have been better?

He had been affectionate, supportive, reassuring and, as she had always known, wonderfully funny and entertaining. He had returned from work early so that she could put her feet up while he had cooked. He had put up with Ellie coming round every few days and had only given her the occasional dry look when her best friend had launched into colourful stories about her love life. He had indulged her sudden taste for soaps on television and brought her cups of tea whenever she wanted. She had been spoiled rotten and that was the problem. It had felt like a *real* relationship. But there was no ring on her finger and she was now terrified that if there was no baby to provide the glue that kept them together, it would all come crashing down around her ears. Had she been too greedy in holding out for perfection?

'I'm going to tell you something, Jennifer, and it may shock you but it needs to be said before Gregory gets here.' James looked at her and felt the ground shift under him. He had always been able to predict the outcome of the things he did and the decisions he made. But then, his biggest decisions had always involved deals and business. He had come to realise that, where emotions were involved, there was no such thing as a predictable outcome, which made it a hell of a lot scarier.

Jennifer braced herself for the shock. She reminded herself that it was better to get it all out of the way.

'If you lose this baby—and I don't think for a minute that you will. In fact, you're probably right, there was probably no need to get Gregory over at all, but better safe than sorry—'

'Just say what you have to say,' she told him gently. 'Between the two of us, I'm the only one allowed to babble when I'm nervous.'

James opened his mouth to tell her that he wasn't

nervous, that nerves were a sign of weakness. Except he *was* nervous.

'Whatever the outcome, I want to marry you, Jennifer. Okay, I'll settle for living together. I don't want to rush you into anything and living together at least gives me a shot at persuading you that we can make this work. But I want to persuade you of that whether or not there's a child involved.'

She looked at him in silence for so long that he began to wonder whether he had got it all wrong. The signs had all been there. Hadn't they? He had a talent for interpreting nuances. Had that talent let him down now?

'We've been happy. You said so yourself.' A defensive tone had crept into his voice.

'Very happy,' she finally whispered, which he thought was a start. She could feel tears begin to gather in the corners of her eyes. Pregnancy had sent her emotions all over the place. Now she wondered whether they had interfered with her hearing as well.

'Are you saying that you want us to be married… whatever…?'

'Whatever.'

'But I don't understand why.'

'Because I can't imagine that there could ever come a day when I wouldn't want to wake up with you next to me, or return from work knowing that you'd be waiting for me. I love you, Jennifer, and, even if you don't return the feeling, I wanted to lay my cards on the table—'

'When you say you *love* me…'

'I love you. With lots of strings attached. So many strings that you'd tie yourself up in knots trying to work your way out of them.'

'I love you too.' She tried to hold back the tremulous grin but failed. 'And what strings are you talking about?'

'I'll tell you later.' The consultant had arrived, a very tall, very gaunt middle-aged man with a severe expression that only relaxed into a smile once his examination was completed and he accepted the cup of tea offered to him.

Some slight concern but nothing to worry about. Blood pressure was a little on the high side but nothing that some rest and relaxation wouldn't sort out. The bleeding would stop and, although he could understand her worry, rest assured that it had not been a dramatic bleed. He had examined and listened and everything was in order. And she was in good hands. He had known James since he was born because he had delivered him.

Jennifer smiled and listened, relieved that her panic had been misguided. Her mind was all over the place. Relief that everything was all right. Wonder mixed with disbelief that James had told her that he *loved her*. Had he just said that because he had thought it might calm her? Had he known that that was what she had wanted to hear? She caught his eye and tried to still the nagging doubts from trying to get a foothold.

Everything in that warm glance he had given her made her heart soar but acceptance of the fact that he didn't love her was so deeply embedded that she was cautious of letting herself get wrapped up in silly dreams.

He could read her mind. The second the consultant had left, he settled her comfortably back on the sofa, tucking the cushions around her and tutting when she told him that she wasn't an invalid.

'I'm not sure I can believe you in any matters to do with health when you decided to keep those giddy spells to yourself,' he chided, and Jennifer half sat up and drew him towards her.

'And I'm not sure I can believe what you said before...'

'I could tell that that was playing on your mind.' He

sighed and pulled one of the chairs towards the sofa and sat on it, taking her hand in his. 'And I don't blame you. I know I made it clear from the start that I wasn't into long-term relationships and I had the history to prove it. My life was my work and I couldn't foresee a time when any woman would take precedence over that. I never realised how big a part you played until you left. I had become accustomed to having you there.'

'I know,' Jennifer said ruefully. 'I always felt like the girl in the background you could relax with but never really looked at. I just saw a procession of gorgeous little blondes and it didn't do anything for my confidence levels. And then I got my degree, got that job in Paris…and best of all, you asked me out to dinner. I thought it was a date. A proper date. I thought you'd finally woken up to the fact that I wasn't a kid any more. I was a woman. I was so excited.'

'And then I knocked you back.'

'I should have known that nothing had changed when you ordered cake and ice cream as a surprise, with a sparkler on top.'

'I'd do the same thing now,' James told her with a slow smile that made her toes curl. 'You love cake and ice cream and I love that about you. I didn't knock you back because of how you looked.'

'It felt that way to me,' Jennifer confessed.

'You were on the brink of going places. When you kissed me, I felt like a jaded old cynic taking advantage of someone young and vital and innocent. You had stars in your eyes. I honestly thought that you deserved better, but it was hard. I'd never touched you before. I was so turned on… We should have had all this out in the open a long time ago.'

'I couldn't. You were right about me. I was very innocent and very young. I wasn't mature enough to handle a discussion about it. I just knew that it felt like the ultimate rejection and I ran away.' She sighed and looked at him tenderly. 'I thought I'd built a new life for myself in Paris and, in a way, I had.'

'You're not kidding. I had the shock of my life when I saw you again at the cottage. You weren't the same girl who'd made a sweet pass at me four years before. I couldn't take my eyes off you.'

'Because I had changed my outward appearance...'

'That's what I thought,' James confessed ruefully. 'I wasn't into the business of exploring my motivations. One and one seemed to add up to two and I took it from there. I never stopped to ask myself how it was that you were the most satisfying lover I'd ever had.'

'Was I? Really?' Jennifer shamelessly prodded him encouragingly and he favoured her with one of those brilliant smiles that could literally make her tummy do somersaults.

'You're fishing.'

'I know. But can you blame me? I spent years daydreaming about you and then just when I thought I'd mastered it, we meet again and I discover that I've always been daydreaming about you. When we finally became lovers... it was the most wonderfully perfect thing in the world.' She thought back to the moment the bubble had burst. 'I never thought for a second that I would get pregnant and the really weird thing was that it was the fault of my condom, the condom I'd bought four years ago...'

'To use with me?' James looked at her in astonishment. 'You're kidding.'

'No, I'm not. I hung onto it for so long that it went past its sell-by date. Actually, I think drowning in salt water and being bashed about in my bag can't have helped prolong its useful life.'

'Well, I'll be damned.'

'When I found out, I had to face up to the truth, which was that you found the sex amazing and you liked me because we'd known each other for such a long time, but you didn't *love* me.'

'The whole business of love was something I hadn't got my head around. I just knew that you turned up holding a bombshell in one hand and a Dear John letter in the other and I couldn't seem to find a way of getting through to you. When I proposed to you, I didn't pause to think that you might actually turn me down.'

'If I'd known…'

'Shall I confess something?'

'What?'

'This house was never renovated to be rented or sold on.'

'What do you mean?'

'It came to my attention because it had been out of action for a while. It must have slipped through the net somewhere along the line but, the second I saw it, I knew I wanted it for you and that was long before I found out that you were pregnant. God, I was a fool. I should have known from the very second I started thinking about you and houses in the same breath that I had fallen in love with you. In fact, I was going to tell you about it when you broke the news.'

Pure delight lit up Jennifer's face and she flung her arms around his neck and pulled him towards her.

'I thought when you dropped all talk about getting married that you were relieved to have been let off the hook… Most men would have been if they found themselves landed with an unwanted pregnancy…'

'Relieved to have been let off the hook?' James laughed and stroked her hair. 'All I could think was that you wanted out, you wanted to be free to find this perfect guy of yours and all I could think was that I needed to put a stop to that, needed to show you that *I* was that perfect guy… I knew that the thought of marriage had sent you into a tailspin. You didn't want to marry me and I wasn't going to try and force your hand and risk you pulling back completely.'

'But I *did* want to marry you. You don't know how much. I just didn't want to be married for the wrong reasons. I hated the thought that you would put a ring on my finger because you couldn't see any other way round the situation. I didn't want to be your lifelong obligation.'

'So now I'm asking you to be the lifelong love of my life. Will you marry me…?'

The wedding was a quiet affair, with family and friends, and, after the scare with the pregnancy, baby Emily was born without any fuss at all. She was plump and pink, with a mop of dark hair, and for both Jennifer and James it was love at first sight.

For a commitment-shy guy determined never to be tamed, James was home promptly every evening. It was very important to delegate, he told her—delegation ensured that employees were kept on their toes and it motivated them in their careers, and if he had taken to working from home now and again, then it was simply because modern technology made it so simple, virtually mandatory in fact.

She would have to get used to having him under her feet because, he further informed her, he was tiring of the concrete jungle. It was no place to bring up all the children he planned on them having. It was a cut-throat world and, besides, there was just so much money a man could use in a lifetime and, that being the case, why waste time

pursuing more when there were so many other, more rewarding things to do with one's time?

And there was no doubt what those other things were.

Jennifer teased him about the man he had become
and she knew that she would spend a lifetime ensur-
ing that the happiness he gave her was returned to him
a thousandfold...

* * * * *

A sneaky peek at next month...

MODERN™

INTERNATIONAL AFFAIRS, SEDUCTION & PASSION GUARANTEED

My wish list for next month's titles...

In stores from 17th August 2012:

- ☐ Unlocking her Innocence – Lynne Graham
- ☐ His Reputation Precedes Him – Carole Mortimer
- ☐ Just One Last Night – Helen Brooks
- ☐ The Husband She Never Knew – Kate Hewitt

In stores from 7th September 2012:

- ☐ Santiago's Command – Kim Lawrence
- ☐ The Price of Retribution – Sara Craven
- ☐ The Greek's Acquisition – Chantelle Shaw
- ☐ When Only Diamonds Will Do – Lindsay Armstrong
- ☐ The Couple Behind the Headlines – Lucy King

Available at WHSmith, Tesco, Asda, Eason, Amazon and Apple

Just can't wait?

Visit us Online

You can buy our books online a month before they hit the shops! **www.millsandboon.co.uk**

0812/0

MILLS & BOON® Book Club

2 Free Books!

Get your free books now at

www.millsandboon.co.uk/freebookoffer

r fill in the form below and post it back to us

E MILLS & BOON® BOOK CLUB—HERE'S HOW IT WORKS: Accepting your e books places you under no obligation to buy anything. You may keep the books d return the despatch note marked 'Cancel'. If we do not hear from you, about a onth later we'll send you 4 brand-new stories from the Modern™ series priced at ,49* each. There is no extra charge for post and packaging. You may cancel at any e, otherwise we will send you 4 stories a month which you may purchase or return us—the choice is yours. *Terms and prices subject to change without notice. Offer id in UK only. Applicants must be 18 or over. Offer expires 31st January 2013. **For terms and conditions, please go to www.millsandboon.co.uk/freebookoffer**

s/Miss/Ms/Mr (please circle) _____

st Name _____

irname _____

ddress _____

_____

_____ Postcode _____

mail _____

end this completed page to: Mills & Boon Book Club, Free Book ffer, FREEPOST NAT 10298, Richmond, Surrey, TW9 1BR

Find out more at
www.millsandboon.co.uk/freebookoffer

Visit us Online

0712/P2YEA

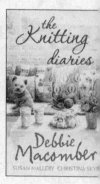